The Queen's Fiction

By
Deji Sowande

In her mind, she's the Queen of the world;
To the world, she's the Queen of the damned.

ISBN: 978-978-943-089-5

Published by LargeHouse

Bear with the typos and grammar in the online chats and emails, they are intentional.

CHAPTER 1

I t was 11.27 p.m., Friday. The night was cool and the sky, hazy. Sparse streetlights dotted the empty dual roads, giving the asphalt surfaces a sort of zebra illumination. Office buildings and big shops, all closed for the day, lined both sides of the road. A cluster of shadows hung around dark alleys, barely illuminated by kerosene lamps. They approached Ogudu roundabout, a zone which barely slept.

A steady 20 hours of daily activity thrived here. A busy taxi and commercial motorcycle park, loud music blared from 70-amp battery-powered audio units wheeled by cart-pushing music bootleggers.

The man stopped the car. His cell phone was almost void of credit. His friend's cell phone needed to be recharged, too. Peering around carefully, he spotted a recharge card retailer. He slid the car towards him and halted close to him, shifting the gear lever to neutral. He couldn't help but cast a furtive glance at the retailer and his stall (a big umbrella under which sat a plastic table and an empty beer crate – the retailer's seat). He understood the city, and in that particular area, he knew one had to be sure whom to patronize, especially at night.

The young card seller was fast. In a flash, he had fetched some cards from his waist pouch.

Over the car radio, a presenter burst into a loud cackle. A call-in show was on, and he was making jest of a caller who just confessed to borrowing clothes from her friends whenever she had a date. The caller joined in the laughter and did her best to respond to the jest. She wouldn't let the presenter have it all because he had control of the studio microphone.

Just as the presenter let a jazz tune overtake their laughter, the man in the car paid the recharge card seller, shifted gear and fed gas into the 6 cylinder-3.0 liter engine. It felt like it had just received an instant shot of gas overdose. Into the free night and darkness ahead, the car sped. Their ride was smooth and the mood, right.

They had spent most of the evening together in his home. She came in at five o'clock, and made dinner, which had formed part of some quality time they'd had in the early evening. And deciding to go clubbing, they were headed for the island.

Clad in a short black satin nightdress, her cleavage was bared, revealing well nurtured skin and the tempting flesh of her fair-sized bust, which heaved sumptuously out of her dress. Her long glossy hair neatly packed across her left shoulder complemented her smile. And she kept fiddling with it, stroking it from her ear down to her bosom. As they descended the avenue into the highway that led to the third mainland bridge, his phone began to ring.

"Hello … hello … I can barely hear you, I'll call back," he said, dropping the phone by the dashboard.

The young woman was engrossed with soft music seeping through the car's speakers and didn't pay him any attention. The phone began to ring again.

"I said I'll call you back," he almost yelled into the mouthpiece the moment he saw it was the same caller.

"You should talk to her. She must be missing you a lot," she calmly advised, facing him with a cynical stare before reclining into her seat and turning away to stare into the dark skies.

"What do you mean?" he asked, shooting her a frown. His voice had just raised a pitch higher.

The phone began to ring once more. This time, she reached it before him and took the call. He moved to seize the phone, but she had engaged the caller in conversation. In just a few seconds, she was yelling into the phone, names and invective shooting into the mouthpiece at such a maddening speed that the man couldn't help but wonder if his companion had suddenly gone psycho. He was sure the caller would be both amazed and perplexed. She or whoever it was had surely gotten more than the intended bargain.

The man was shocked, caught between snatching the phone off her palm, driving the car and managing his squalling lover. With her attention slit between the heavy phone rage and the struggle for its possession, her aggravation hit its peak. And sliding down her window, she hurled the phone into the lagoon.

"What the fuck … are you out of your mind?" he sparked, screaming at the top of his deep voice.

She simply ignored him. Arms folded across her chest, she reclined into her seat, giving its lever a sharp pull, which tilted it backwards. Relaxed, she focused to just stare straight at the long bridge ahead. Anger welled in him. And in a flash, he grabbed her left arm with his thick right hand, shook her vigorously and shoved her roughly against the car door.

"I'll make sure you pay for this, bitch!" he yelled at her.

She went mad, practically flew into a rage. His anger was too sudden and unexpected.

"Fuck you! Shameless cheat!" she almost spat at him. Banging wildly, her fists expressed her anger as they hit the dashboard, her feet kicking around aimlessly.

"You're not worth it at all. I shouldn't have had anything to do with you in the first place…

You're no different from a baboon… Uncultured idiot! I hate you! I never knew you!"

The man shut up. Just then, peace reigned. Or was it stillness? He calmed down, and she glowed, an instant sense of satisfaction consuming her. Yes! She had won. And then she noticed… the car had stopped.

Why? She wondered.

They were just halfway across the 11-kilometer bridge, and the engine went dead. He had killed it, removed the key and calmly stepped out of the

2003 Toyota Camry. Walking to her side of the car, he opened the door, and with his six-foot-four-inch heavily built body, he grabbed her by an arm and a leg and dragged her out of her seat. Against his very strong masculine frame, her fight was frail; with all her body involved, she couldn't remain in the car.

Eventually, he pulled her out of the car, carrying her struggling slim mass in both arms. With a foot, he shut the door, stepped some yards behind the car and threw her with no care onto the coarse road. He didn't bat an eyelid, not with oncoming vehicles speeding toward them. Back to the car, he slipped into his seat.

Fear lit up her eyes even in the dark night. Swiftly, as much as his stunning actions could permit her, she staggered back up and limped off the main tracks. She was very terrified. An oncoming vehicle could have crushed her. She clutched her tummy and rose swiftly to rush to him, but he had locked the zoomed off. She bent down, holding her knee with her hands, and gazed at the fading taillights of the Camry. She was in pains. Not just pains from her outburst but also from her left leg and waist. The side of her left knee was bruised, and she had winced from the sharp pain that shot through her body the moment she had landed on her waist. Her short temper had just cost her some hurting price, and she hated herself for it.

At the verge of tears, she peered into the darkness. The car's taillights were growing bigger. She could see the car backing up toward her and she sighed. Some relief… Then she straightened and stood to watch what would happen next, a forced smile on her face.

Maxwell halted the car six yards beside Queen, rolled down the front passenger window, flung her bag into her face and bolted into the night.

***

The five-foot-nine slim figure walked into class in her six-inch heeled shoes.

I love my new Prada shoes. She kept telling herself as she picked her strides with little care.

Bet they're all wishing they were me... bitches and haters. I'll always be on top while they remain at the bottom of the food chain. They will only fantasize about being me.

Ever so confident, she was looking really different that day, the same way she did each time she remembered the need to be in school. Most of her classmates beefed her – the girls mostly. The guys burned in lust... there was no way in the world any of them would ask her for a date; she was way beyond their reach.

It was 8 a.m. Monday morning, and the classroom was packed full. It was obvious there was an important test. She can't miss that one for any reason, not for her own funeral. A 200-seater classroom cramped up with over 400 students, some hanging by the windows and the walls. Those that managed to get seats had to be in class two hours early.

Tightly clustered against each other, eight to ten students sat on benches and desks meant for five occupants. In this unfortunate situation, some still managed to keep spaces for friends that were yet to arrive. Plenty of noise filled the already heated air, everyone catching up on the events of the weekend.

Last Saturday was a champion's league final. The underdogs had beaten the defending champion four goals to nothing. On Sunday, a woman had given birth to a dog during a church prayer session. There was plenty of gist, *breaking news* as it had come to be baptized on campus. Boys had football argument, and superstitious sentiments held the girls spellbound.

The air was tight from inadequate ventilation, and the ceiling fans barely worked; a few rotating in lazy drones interrupted often by slight creaking that often raised goose bumps on a few skins. The classroom wasn't actually designed for this crowd. Thanks to the sorry lecturer who believed the true test of a student's performance is in deducting 20 marks by default from the accumulation of tests, assignments and exam. This resulted in mass spilling; he prided himself with producing 10-year-old spills.

Rumour had it that it took him three extra years to graduate from the free education his generation enjoyed in their time, making him pay back for his misfortune. The school senate had summoned him several times over allegations of misconduct, but his argument had always been that the students were too lazy with his course and wouldn't commit to adequate research.

As she made her way through the thickness of the crowded room, most eyes shifted to her, and instantly she became the subject of the gossip. Dense pathways suddenly became broad walkways for her.

With a little hiss here and a little gossip there, amidst an aura of hypocrisy, hate and lust, she completed her entry. And finally, she spotted her best bud, K.C., in her regular spot. Beside K.C., the young lady took a reserved space, and K.C.'s face lit up. They hugged, with gesticulations.

"Hello!" Queen hailed, excited at seeing her friend.

"Hey girlfriend, you look smashing today. I want to be like you when I grow up!"

She adored her friend so much and always held her as a source of inspiration in the world of fashion and socializing. Queen had successfully paired her with a couple of her male friends, and she was having a good time so far. They had met during registration in their freshman year but hadn't really struck out as friends back then; they had different orientations.

Kelechi was of academic background. Her dad was a professor at the University of Lagos; mom, the Dean of some department in the state university. The firm grip from her folks always kept her in check to some extent, but she tried out a little adventure at every available open window.

A cute, petite girl, she was the type that grew into high-caliber executive positions, someone who knew her onions, capable of studying an alien subject and sitting her exams at short notice.

She was the pride of her parents, their only child. Her parents were very focused in their individual careers and lavished all the love they could accommodate on her. Kelechi's dreams were big, and her aspirations way too unimaginable.

"Liar," Queen replied, trying to make her friend feel good about herself, too. "Why is the big fool not here yet?"

"Dunno."

"Bet you are prepared – you know I've got a blockhead. Besides, I didn't sleep last night, Onyx rocked… met this big boy that's hooking me up with some cheez soon… The guy's so loaded you can smell it in his breath." Queen chuckled, "Girlfriend, I'm not lucky. I'm just blessed!"

"Cool," K.C. answered, "You're the best at sniffing out the loaded guys, I'm still on your tutelage and I'm loving it… chilling till my folks are on holidays again. I'll make money, too. Meanwhile, don't worry about the test, we'll be fine. Besides, he repeats questions and I'm sure you'll be able to pass on your own."

"Me? Pass a test… on my own? Girlfriend, why the tease? Remind me that I'm dumb and I'll at least smile," she giggled.

K.C joined her in giggling.

***

At the parking lot, Ace was waiting patiently in his black nicely-pimped baby boy-a Honda Accord 2001. With low profile tyres, black alloyed wheels, high-tech woofers in the booth and enhanced engine improved with turbo charge, the car looked menacingly appealing.

One thing about this particular car is that it was the most used among guys in his profession back in the days; guys believed to be in the hustle. It was very popular among them as they tried to emulate the main character – Tyrese Gibson – of a popular African American 2001 movie *Baby Boy*. At 21, Ace still had a lot of attachment to that era, the movie being his best. He was very relaxed with his seat reclined as he listened to Lil Wayne's Carter II, his best album ever.

His cell phone's ring tone, *Tony Montana*, a popular song in Lagos, soothingly played on his phone. He smirked, checked the screen and took the call. That killed the music. With a feigned accent trying to sound Caucasian, he said, "Hello beautiful, sleep good?"

"Yea, I did, but I miss you so much."

"I miss you too, honey. You're the best thing to have happened to a lost soul like me," Ace acknowledged. "I picked up the Western Union, darling. It came at the right time, and I made the payment about an hour ago. Everything will be just fine."

"OK, honey, I'm just so bothered about you," came Stacey's excited voice through the speaker.

"You're my everything... my whole life is wrapped up around you."

"I know, baby, same here."

"Can't wait till you're back home... wanna murder you with love. This distance is killing me!"

"It's harder for me, babe."

"Yea, but babe, you go conquer the world and bring home the spoils of war. Bahamas on my mind!"

"Sure, sweetheart, this die-hard brute is sucking 'em dry out here and bringing all the riches for her majesty's retirement."

Just then, Ace spotted Queen and K.C. as they walked towards his car. Placing an index finger on his lips while he continued his conversation with Stacey, he signaled them to keep their voices down. The two gorgeous ladies opened a door each and closed them gently, avoiding unneeded noise while they stayed mute. Queen's gesture clearly spelled her pride for him, and that earned him a peck on the cheek. She turned to look at her friend who was already tucked into the seat behind her.

"He's my boy," she whispered.

K.C. agreed with a nod.

Ace rounded up his conversation assuring Stacey he was working on fine-tuning the concluding part of his business in Africa. He also assured her of his undying love for her and how far he would go to make her happy for the rest of her life.

Then he turned to K.C.

"Hi…"

For Queen, it was a passionate kiss. Her face turned a little red while K.C. turned to stare out of the window, acting not bothered while wishing they were in alternate seats.

***

In the slums of Lagos – Mushin actually – at a beer parlor, young men in their late teens and early twenties were gathered, dancing to disquieting noise blaring from poorly built speakers while they sang along to some popular Naija music.

Mushin was a popular slum, notorious as a breeding ground for thugs and thieves back in the '80s and '90s. It also was birthplace to a lot of Nigerian athletes, mostly boxers. The slum was home to a popular market and some other commercial centers. Back in the days, the best street fighters around here were demigods to young boys. Stories of street fights and inter-hood wars were legendary tales in high schools around Lagos. Mushin was generally known for its major involvement in new trends of ills in the society.

There was hardly any noticeable change in the neighborhood, but for banks and a few companies that had sprung up over the years. It used to be a very dirty environment until the new state governor, with a consciousness for orderliness and cleanliness, saw to its facelift, the same virtues which most parts of Lagos were also wearing.

Now, Mushin had become the celebrated home of Internet fraud, a choice home to the not-so-successful, lowly fraudsters. Guys from here were usually underdogs who had bosses in town.

In time they got to know the game better due to the fraternity between the younger out-of-school boys and college undergraduates.

***

At The Spot, one of the few most popular beer zones, boys were busy drinking beer. Some were on the dance floor, others were seated in their numbers with burning weed in glaring display while others smoked cigarettes. That was regular scenery in the very remote parts of Mushin.

Ace came along, his girls with him, and the excitement within The Spot rose sharply. Ace was a commander no doubt. His presence always heralded more fun – wine, women and weed.

"You don't come around our hood as you used to, Mr. Ace. It would do us all a lot of good if you carry us along your path to riches. I got your back always, my brother from another mother," Biggie blurted out, grabbing Ace's hand with both of his and pumping it hardly in a revered handshake. He was hardly able to control his surging excitement. He was already high.

"I'm so sorry, bro, I've been really busy," Ace apologized. And he meant it. He knew he was lord to most guys around town.

Biggie was some guy who couldn't write a single correct English sentence, a high school dropout who ended up a thug. His anger was dreaded among all *area boys* in Mushin. He had a notorious reputation for getting instantly provoked over nothing and tearing the object of his provocation apart in a flash. Best relayed, his nickname was *Havoc!*

Ace knew that Biggie led a gang of street urchins who muscled cuts from commercial bus drivers daily and delivered returns to the big guys (fighters who rose in rank in the transportation underworld.) Biggie's record was bad. He had been involved in lots of blood-curdling crimes, so much that every new cop posted to

Mushin had to study his profile and graciously accept the Divisional Police Head's instruction to always endeavour to steer clear of the hoodlum's path. For such an inhuman fellow who had done a murder rap – eleven straight months – in a maximum-security prison and still found himself free on the streets, drug dealing, street gambling and armed robbery were just kiddies' lessons for greenhorns.

During his murder trial, the state prosecutor had established his case against Biggie beyond all reasonable doubt. With a pocket axe, he had hacked a young man to death over a non-issue, a murder that had triggered a series of area fights that raged for many days. The judge had committed him to prison. But people were yet to understand how he returned to the streets barely eleven months after his sentence. Even with the victim's family sworn to vengeance.

Ace dreaded this killer.

With his 96 kilograms and 5-foot-10 body, his agility could pass for that of a professional sprinter. These days, he had become a top dog in Mushin, a kingpin in fake check rackets. He supplied checks to guys from town. Often, he would sell in bulks of between 100 to 2,000 notes for 7,000 naira per hundred. And he could offer a discount on purchases in arithmetic progression. He could also give out between one to five checks – sure checks, as they were popularly named – to his best customers in return for a percentage on profit from the transaction it was used for.

Ace sure knew all these. So he knew who to never attempt to ignore. With Biggie, such attitude could mean trouble.

"Damn! You ladies are so beautiful and quite different from the stock we got in this hood. It seems you guys dropped from the sky," Biggie lamented in his high-pitched tone. "I must not settle for less, I will marry me a pretty woman."

"How are you, fine girl?" he turned to K.C., stretching his thick hand for a handshake.

"I'm OK," she answered and obliged him the handshake with visible reluctance, laced with fear. She could imagine his big hand slapping her face.

"How are you?" he greeted again, repeating the same gesture with Queen.

"I'm all right," she answered too.

"Find me a friend like you… I will take her round the world and buy her a Jeep," Biggie swore with a wry smile.

"Don't worry, sir. I will find you a pretty girl," she agreed in deceit.

"Sit down there, y'all," Biggie ushered them to empty seats around his table. His tongue could hardly cease its wagging. And it continually splattered spittle all over. The girls were really not comfortable with him and the environment. They wondered what transactions a cultured guy like Ace would have with such guys.

Diversion came. A fat, tall woman backing an unkempt child walked up to them, "Kilemamu," she asked. *What will you drink?*

"Smirnoff Ice for the babes, Star Lager for me," Ace quickly ordered and turned to Biggie.

"Nothing."

As they got settled in, Biggie summoned Ace to a corner. "What's up, chairman, did you come with the bar?"

"Of course, big man," Ace replied and handed him a chunk of green bills. Eyes gleaming with excitement, Biggie counted the bills and smiled.

"Correct!" he exclaimed, "You are correct, boy, two Gs is the sure way to go." Ace caught a surprise, though short-lived. He didn't expect that Biggie would grab him in a sudden bear hug. But he did and pulled him back to their table.

"More beer for everybody," Biggie shouted to the bartender. "More beer, there is money!"

***

Next morning at the gates of a factory, a frail old man with a face moulded out of years of agony and poverty moved to and from his post to open the gates for inward and outward bound vehicles. This he did in turn with his lifelong friends, his fellow guards who doubled as his foes and family. He had known them for two decades.

Gossip all day – that was essentially all they did. And for old men with no concrete hope for the next meal, it seemed to be a befitting pastime. The men cherished their relationship although it had all grown on falsehood and hatred but later began to be nurtured by their coexistence. They survived on tips from the company's visitors.

In their dingy cubicle, security overalls hung on barely painted walls. Two old batons hung from nails on the wall, and on a big old plain-topped, termite-ridden desk were a couple of worn-out writing pads, a tattered bible and a freshly-used eating bowl.

"These politicians are so unpredictable. Imagine this Adamson boy, he swaps parties like he changes shirts. These people are so greedy they have swept integrity to the gutters. That boy was my private in the army. I was so good to him back then, but now he knows me no more. If it weren't for me, he wouldn't be where he is today. I introduced him to the captain in my platoon, and he made Adamson his driver. He has since been posted to various missions and promoted rapidly."

"The boy is just plain lucky," his first colleague countered.

"I went to see him twelve years ago, but he wouldn't grant me audience. I felt like trash that day. I actually trained this boy," Queen's father bragged.

"You sound like you handpicked him and placed him where he is today, old fool," his squat second colleague fired at him, "You'd better shut up and face your work… dreamer."

***

"Big fool, look at you… You don't know the capital of Czech is Prague? And that's where I'll spend my holidays when my ship sails in. It's one of the most beautiful cities in the world," Queen declared.

"You feel on top of the world because you know one thing that I don't. Your total brain functionality is less than five percent of mine – hope you know that. I'm the king of the world and the most brilliant fraudster on earth."

"There you go again, blabber… Like you know it all! I hate men that brag; they end up being nothing. If you weren't a cute boy, I would have chosen to be with men who would appreciate me better and treat me like I deserve."

"Who says you can't? Like I always tell you, the door's open to whoever wishes to come in or leave."

"Yeah… right, Mr. Confidence, you'll cry at losing me someday. I'm the finest there is. You'll never find yourself a chic like me. Ama leave your sorry ass someday, and you're gonna cry."

"Like I care, bitch… This boy is sexy and he's a bloke. I got money, a duffle bag full of benjamins."

"Paper, paper, paper, all I get is paper. Green paper, white chalk yellow tape will … Ama grind till I drop. Y'all bitches know I'm da boss, the Teflon don, the Aston Martin man," Queen raps along with him.

"Babe, I'm the best there is, so don't test me. You'll always be my girl and you know it. Nothing will break me and my Queen. All I need in this life of sin is me and my girlfriend," he sang out loud.

"Down to ride till the very end is me and my boyfriend," Queen replied in the same song style.

They both rapped and sang at length, with passion in their eyes, and swayed. Then, Ace grabbed her with his skinny limbs and drew her into his bosom. Posting kisses on every available spot on her neck, his lips moved up and he nibbled on her ear, licking it. She moaned. His hand moved deftly, and her tits took some generous squeezing. Her nipples accepted the whole pressure, and she was already soaring into the unknown.

Swiftly, Ace pushed her to a wall, and she supported herself with her hands just in time before he bent her over and pulled her jeans down to her ankles in a somewhat vicious manner. She shrieked as he rammed into her… they did it like they both enjoy it. Crashing around, she kept shrieking, moaning, objecting and shouting like it was a wrestle. Then, just the same way it began, it ended. The duo passed out on a sofa.

***

8 o'clock the next morning, a loud pounding came on the living room's door. Inquisitively, Ace asked if Queen was expecting anyone. She wasn't, she replied. Ace rushed to the door and peeped through his makeshift spyhole, which he had personally bored through the big wooden door.

His guests' faces were unfamiliar. He rushed back into his bedroom to Queen with his penis dangling.

"5.0!" he whispered, "Stay put and gimme two seconds." In a dash, he was in his room to tidy up. And in a flash, he headed back to the door having asked

Queen to remain the way she was with sheets covering her hot nude body.

All this happened in less than 200 seconds.

"Who be that?" he questioned, shouting at the people on the other side of the door.

With a feigned voice, a lady answered, "It's me, Precious."

So as not to sound leery, he opened the door. To his expectation, five uniformed policemen, two plainclothes men and a lady appeared, some wielding guns. They ushered him back into his apartment.

His face was an instant mask ridden with queries.

Ace, confident his incriminating items were properly concealed, made a move to keep them off the thoroughfare, but they still muscled their way in. Being law enforcement agents, they threatened to shoot him if he should attempt any mischief. But Ace wasn't bugged. And he didn't budge. He understood police gimmicks. They'd always rub their authority in your face.

Queen pretended to be unaware of the situation and woke up as one of the cops tapped her on the shoulder. Her eyes dilated on the seeing the cop's gun, and she went cold. Just a fairly good act because she feigned it as if she just got wind of their presence.

"Wake up, ashawo *(whore)*. Una dey work together, abi? *(You're his accomplice, right?)*"

"There's a petition on you guys at our station. We have orders from Force Headquarters, Abuja to search this home. Your operations will be terminated today, and I will personally make sure you guys rot in jail," the corporal in the team blurted out.

"You can't do nothing," Ace replied reassuringly, "And leave my girl alone. I'm the one you're looking for, not her."

The next male cop stepped closer and tapped Queen on the butt. That earned him a slap from her. It had been out of reflex, but she barely feared his reaction. She quickly moved to one end of the couch, clutching the sheets tightly. The cop grabbed it and almost yanked it off.

"Halt!" the lady cop barked. And that was Queen's saving grace. The man would have bared her nudity before the pack as payback.

"Get out and go into the van, now!" the lady cop barked again, and the cop instantly felt sorry.

In his anger, the cop nudged Ace out of his way as he made his exit. Ace, who would never be bullied, no, not in his own home, moved to fight him but got a grip on his temper the moment the lady cop stepped before him.

"Oga *(boss)*, let's begin our search on this foolish boy's house. He's a big criminal… heard he has built two houses from this *yahoo* business," said the third male cop.

But Savage had her plan. She summoned Ace to a corner of the room and signaled Queen to get dressed. The two-bedroom apartment was tastefully furnished and cozy. Ace sure knew how to live the good life. Two parallel walls shared the same color; one was red and the other dove-grey. His leather settee was golden-brown, a classy look that accentuated the room's aesthetics. A big 47-inch television hanging three feet from the floor had a big white woofer underneath. His home theater player, PS3 and decoder were neatly arranged in a coffee-brown closet with a transparent glass door. This sat at the wall's angle.

Between the big sofa and the electronics stand was a crystal center table, which sat on a thick woolen center carpet. Besides these few items, the big living room was lavished with plenty of space.

"Where is your computer, young man?" Savage asked, "See me as your mum, ehn?"

Ace giggled.

"My mum indeed!" he muttered inaudibly, stifling some laughter.

"I really do not like the idea of you being harassed, especially in the presence of the beautiful lady you have in your nice home. I want you to cooperate with me so that we can leave you in peace and not cause you further embarrassment," Savage offered calmly, though she sounded very unconvincing.

Ace kept mum, pretending to have bought her false tale. The lady cop laid a hand on his shoulder and…

"We actually got a report from Abuja that you are a *yahoo* kingpin."

That was Madam Savage! She won't hesitate to hit a target with seeming A-class information. It was her usual intimidating gimmick. Becky Savage had become notorious in the force for her fierceness and wits. She was believed to have faced a gang of robbers alone with her 22mm revolver. Strategically positioned, she disrupted a major bank operation, killing three heavily armed robbers before backup got to the scene. This happened 12 years ago.

Since then, she had risen in rank and been appointed to handle strategic jobs. And her colleagues lived with not just reverence for her but fear. Sheer, broad daylight fear! None could predict her antics. She could employ anything to score her goal any time.

Even in the underworld, her reputation had gone viral. To hear *'Savage'* in any Lagos neighbourhood meant some crooks had to either go underground fast or end up in chains. At 5-foot-4, she had been slender in her glory days but now a little oversized with potbelly from childbearing, beer and pepper soup.

"I can assure you of total security and protection in this job. I like you. You're a good-looking young man, someone with focus and discipline. If you will own up to me, I will make sure you are very fine."

More warmly she approached him again. "I have a son like you who is very ambitious, too, and I would like him to meet you someday. You guys can do business together. Be a good boy, eh? Talk to mommy."

"Madam... thank you for your talk," Ace answered and cunningly bowed his head to show his respect for the woman. "You're a correct person, ma."

"Thank you, my son."

"I'm not pleased with the bombardment of my private life. Honestly, I'm not a *yahoo* boy. I'm just a fortunate young man with a magic wand."

He stared straight into Savage's eyes searching for weakness.

"Seriously, if you search the whole of my house, you'll find nothing. I like it that you called me to the side, which I respect so much. I'm also happy that you didn't allow your boy to shame my girlfriend. Please give me your number and take mine. I want you to send me your account number as soon as you get to the office, and you will get an alert from your bank before the end of the day," he dropped.

The cop gang just watched.

Now holding her hand, Ace said, "Trust me, you'll smile when you see the amount."

"Ace, Ace…" Savage hailed him, searching his mind, "I've heard a lot about you," she informed him, wearing a big grin. "You are as good at toasting as you are with *yahoo*. You've got a very sweet mouth. How do you expect me to believe your little speech, small boy?"

Ace smiled. He loved the notion of word about him in town.

"Even if I was the only one that came, do you think I will leave here empty-handed?" Madam Savage asked. "Hell no, not with these angry boys I came with," she declared, shifting her gaze from Ace to her teammates. Ace followed her gaze. The men had begun a drinking party. From his fridge, they had made themselves comfortable with beer and liquor. Queen sat on the sofa, hating and cursing under her breath.

"Are you OK with that?" Savage asked Ace. "Would you want them to take your home apart? Right now…" she added.

"I don't see any need for all that, ma'am," Ace whimpered. The whole scenario was already hitting his nerves, filling him with a sour taste.

"No there's need… ample need. We could raise a score of evidence here, right now. And you'd be sorry," she declared, finality in her tone.

"There's nothing, I assure you. But if you insist on searching, well… I tell you it will just be another routine search. Wasted time on your side…"

"We'll find nothing?"

"You'll find nothing!" Ace insisted.

"Then, let's try. Boys!"

All cops smarten up.

"Gosh!" Ace exclaimed, "You just wanna delay me. I'm running late already."

"Sorry, boy, we met you in bed," Savage hit at him. "Now, come here…"

Farther away, she pulled him aside, and they chatted for some three minutes and finally agreed on something. They exchanged digits, and Savage stared him fixedly into both eyes.

"I believe you've heard about me and you know what I am capable of doing. I will not take shit from you and I will personally make sure you are jailed if you fuck up."

"I will not fuck up, madam."

"You know me well, e? I'll give you just one chance. Make sure you see me at the office so we can talk better. I will introduce you to the commissioner of police and I will make sure you are safe from police harassment."

She stretched her hand and held him on the shoulder, bending him over, "You're a nice young man, e? Keep it up and take care of my beautiful young lady. OK?"

Off she stormed out of the house. And her boys joined her.

Ace walked to Queen instantly and squeezed her in a tight hug. The whole episode had got him a bit ruffled.

"Ignore the bastards, Sugarplum. They're just a bunch of hungry motherfuckers. I'm sorry about the foolish one that touched you. You know I'll never let anyone hurt you. I'm so sorry, baby."

"It's OK, Ace, you didn't ask for it. They're just hungry fools like you said. They've got no business with you, honey," Queen replied warmly, cuddling him.

After a long session of cuddling and kissing, Ace spoke, "Let's freshen up and go out!"

Ace drove her to an uptown restaurant, somewhere nice and quiet, and they had a good meal. Afterwards, he paid 50,000 naira into Savage's account.

CHAPTER 2

Brenda sat on the right side of the back seat of a 2010 Honda CRV, her official car. She is smartly dressed in her coffee brown Hugo Boss skirt suit, light brown shoes, Louis Vuitton handbag, black Gucci wristwatch, glossy cream shirt and oyster necklace. She smelled really good. She made it a duty to dress well always. She earned a lot and barely had any responsibility but to look good and make money for her bank.

She had been on the job since graduating four years ago. She started as a teller and was very hardworking, until some boss from the head office noticed her on an inspection visit. The boss noticed the rare beauty Brenda possessed, tall and lanky with full cleavage and moderately protruding curves.

She's the dream and hurt of a man, what thrills him and kills him, were the words of the lady who spotted her. *I will groom her and make her the best!*

That was how the money-making machine BRENDA was created. She had been a good student all through university and graduated with first-class. An easy communicator, she had big, cat-like eyes that turned a man feeble when locked on her gaze. She was really beautiful.

"First rule, never sleep with a client," Ms. Jaga informed Brenda. "Do that and you lose your dignity as a woman. You'll lose your pride and command for respect. But lure them, make passes at them, make them yearn for you, kiss them on the cheek, touch them at the tip of their nose, do all the preambles," she added sweetly but then suddenly barked, "All I need is the cash!"

Brenda stepped out of the car and walked up a flight of stairs to the landing of the giant glass entrance. The great doors gave way to her as she got close to them. Then she walked into the lobby of one of the leading mobile networks in Nigeria. Heads turned. Who would see her and not steal a second look? Her enchanting appearance was a stigma to men.

"Sir, Miss Brenda is here to see you," a plump, 34-year-old assistant announced to her boss. She was uncomfortable with Brenda's presence. Her first and last visits hadn't been good ones between them. She felt intimidated by Brenda and tried to play bossy, oblivious of the importance of the beautiful woman's visit. Her boss, Emeka, had warned her severely of her nonsensical welcome of the big visitor.

"Please ask her to come right in," Emeka replied, with obvious anticipation.

"I'll be thanking you for your observation sir, and I am giving you my word that adjustments will be made ASAP." He rose to his feet and abruptly ended a non-conclusive discussion with his aging client.

"We'll have to schedule another meeting. There's an issue that requires urgent attention, sir. I hope you'll bear with me, sir," Emeka stretched forth a hand to the 60-something-year-old man who, in turn, shook his hand in bewilderment as he also rose to his feet.

"I will have my assistant work with yours to fix another date," the old man said, a tone of disappointment in his voice. "Thank you very much, Mr. Emeka."

"You're always welcome, sir," Emeka replied, adjusting himself behind the departing old man.

The gorgeous lady walked in. "Good day, sir," she saluted the old man, who returned the gesture.

"Hello, young lady."

These young people lack courtesy he intoned. *They probably want to have a good time. How does the fool expect to achieve a lot in life when he mixes business with pleasure?* He shut the door behind him.

"How are you doing, Brenda? You're 20 minutes early. It's really good to see you!"

"Thank you, Emeka, how's the family?"

"We're doing fine."

He walked towards her before she got to his desk, shook her hand and ushered her to an antique sofa. They sat at either end of the comfortable piece of relic. Emeka had a taste for classic stuff. He personally designed his office and had most of the furnishings shipped in from an antique road show he had visited in the U.K. Very unusual in the Nigerian scene, he still kept his father's 1962 Mercedes-Benz. He had it shipped to the U.S. for an overhaul when he became a Lagos Big Boy. He drove this unusual but grand car only to very important functions, the kind of occasions where he would be seen driving in. He always ensured he was seen in it; he loved to make an entrance.

"Is my check ready, bros?"

"Yes, it is."

"Good. Can I have it?" Brenda demanded, sounding firm and unperturbed.

"Yes, you will, but I have instructions from the BABA."

"What will that be? This is harvest time, isn't it?"

"Brenda…"

"Yes, please."

"Baba has a check of eight million naira for you. He's on a working holiday to Bahrain and hopes it will cover your travel expenses. Exact dates I will personally send to your phone by text."

"Emeka… we've been over this a thousand times. Can I have my check, please?"

"Sure," he answered, standing up. He walked to his desk and returned in 24 seconds with the check.

"Here we go, beautiful."

Brenda took the check, placed it neatly in a diary she produced from her bag and rose to her feet. Emeka also rose up, swallowing saliva.

"Brenda," he called and paused for a second, "You know you're always on my mind…"

Brenda cut him short. "Please bros, I gotta go."

"Erm…" he mumbled a few inaudible words.

But she was gone already, out the door.

***

Queen found her way to an Aboki *(local exchange bureau)* and exchanged the $800 she got from Ace for its naira equivalent. She bought some accessories and makeup and hailed a cab to take her home. Traffic was heavy on the outskirts of Lagos, where she was residing with her folks, where she grew up… precisely Ikorodu.

She stopped at a local market, bought groceries, got back in the cab and rode some minutes.

"Aunty Kaosara!" A couple of kids screamed, gathering in excitement on seeing her. It was a norm in such poor neighborhoods for kids, most of them living in squalor, to initiate a rowdy welcome for their *aunties* every time they met one. It also paid them. The kids ran to her and took her bags. Her street was a long one. Most folks were not into nine- to-five around here. Many were traders and artisans who simply lazed around. At this time of the day, plenty were at home engaged in their usual pastime... gossip.

Queen sure knew how to show her regards for elders. And as she walked down the street, she couldn't help but pause to exchange greetings. Her family's home was a two-room affair. In buildings such as the one housing their home, there was a hallway with rooms on both sides of the stretch. The single-story building was home to some 23 families. In it were a central toilet and bathroom area behind the building. Every household had to use the little space beside the door of their apartment as kitchen.

Kaosara – her birth name, not particularly palatable – christened herself Queen in high school, although neighbors still preferred her original name. She had realized her good looks early in life, but it had caused her a lot of trouble with both the boys in the hood and at school. Love never crossed her mind, as she grew up in a no-love zone. She had managed to patch up her life with the few good men she had met, men who had encouraged her to get an education and endeavor to become someone of good value in life. She did follow their counsel, although it was somewhat pressured. She never loved school, and her entrance exams to the university were passed by hook. Her body bought her way through everything. Queen had been hurt countless times and was unhappy with life, though she cared little about her misfortunes.

She had to move on and become someone. Her only life aspiration was to meet that one loaded guy that would pay all her bills and those of her family. She still thought like a '70s girl with the carriage of today's girls.

She managed to speak like the uptown girls, since she mingled with a lot of them. She was very choosy with the company she kept. If you listened carefully, you'd notice the glitch in her intonation, but you'd already be too carried away by her looks and availability. She was a mindreader. Queen could tell what you were thinking and she knew if you were worth getting a piece of her. Her slogan was *no pleasure without pay*.

Into her family apartment, she entered and was met by her excited mom.

"Queen, Queen," her mom hailed her, having succumbed to her daughter's insistence on being addressed by her self-christened name. Queen had been the main source of livelihood in the family for some time. She called the shots.

"How are you? You dey enjoy oo," *(You are enjoying o.)* her mom said in admiration of her daughter.

"Thank you, maami," Queen smiled her appreciation. The kids had to be settled first.

"Take. It's for all of you."

"Yeeee…" the kids could barely hold their joy. They'd just earned 500 naira.

"Share it well o," Queen advised them, nudging them towards the door. It was a common thing with the kids to struggle for control. Queen was unconcerned, though. Behind them, she shut the door.

"I love your hair, Queen. This one is different," Mom complimented her.

"Of course it is – and very expensive, too."

"I see it is… how much is it?" she asked with a child's inquisitiveness.

"You don't want to know, Mom."

Her mother insisted.

"Only 120k," Queen dropped.

"Kaosara!" Mom screamed, "Why are you doing this to yourself? That money will start you up in good business. It's better to make sensible choices, my child."

"You don't know what's in vogue. This is new age, Mom."

"Where's everybody?"

"Your father's at work, and your brothers are in school."

"Good, Mommy, let me quickly give you what I brought before Dad gets back," she said and brought out 70,000 naira.

"Please keep it safe and don't let Papa know. I know the rent will expire soon. Save toward it and support Daddy if he doesn't have enough."

"I will, my daughter. Thank you very much. God will bless you."

They talked into the evening and also made dinner from the groceries Queen came home with.

***

Late night at a bar around the University of Lagos, a few boys were seated and drinking, three of them armed with tools for the night. Their gist was about past successful operations, girls, cars and moneymaking. Impatiently, they awaited word from the boss. The oldest among them would be about twenty years old. With an air of anxiety, the loud music, the coolness of the night and intoxication from alcohol, they made indiscriminate noise, shouting at the top of their voices to be audible under loud Naija music.

At 11.30, Banji's phone rang. He stood to his feet and walked far from the music. He picked it up and punched some digits on his other phone. He summoned two of the guys to him and gave them individual digits and locations. The other guys just stared at them, longing to know what was going on. Banji continued to give instructions to the two guys, and in two minutes they were done.

"Time don reach, let's bounce!" *(It's time, let's go!)*

The involved parties got in three different cars and drove off. Others remained, attending to their drinks. They talked about what levels the active boys were into and how they could get a piece of the free cake.

On each tool were three boys. Two of them attended to one ATM while one sat in the car with the engine running. 11.55 p.m., they slotted in their cards and punched in pin codes. Sixty pieces of $100 bills spilled from the machine. They wore victorious smiles, picked the cash and dashed into their cars. They immediately drove to other ATMs and repeated their act. At ten minutes past midnight, they were all together again at Banji's appointed location.

Banji collected 60 percent of each team's loot, got into his Volkswagen Touareg and drove into the night. Later that morning, Banji delivered $10,800 – 30 percent of the loot – to Bros's wife in Victoria Island.

Bros was a fraud kingpin based in the U.K. He was believed to be making a minimum of $150,000 weekly in recent times with the new scam mode in town. He had built an empire for himself from bank transfers, check frauds and other loose ends that brought in cash. He had a big network of guys working for him around the globe. Bros was a very shrewd businessman, very direct.

Banji knew Bros from childhood. Bros used to work with his dad until Bros eloped with his father's 750,000 naira, which he used to buy his travel to the U.K. in 2002. He had paid back the money with unbelievable interest, and a healthy relationship had since been reconciled. Banji had been the most beneficial from this relationship. He controlled a lot of Bros's businesses in Nigeria.

Once, Banji had gone on an errand for Bros in South Africa and came back to Nigeria with his own $70,000. Banji was a very big boy and one of the pacesetters in his school. He belonged to a prestigious club and had plenty of girls on his chain. Banji was a big mouth, very cocky and loved to flaunt his cash.

At 20, he had probably handled more cash of his own than could be imagined. He had chartered a plane and flown 200 friends to Ghana for some wild party, all expenses paid. He had been living in a three-star hotel for 16 months and regularly took extra rooms when friends came around. He was with a different girl every other day and he was notorious for making good girls go bad.

There was a new leak those days and he was very in the know.

It's time to step up my game, he thought to himself. *It's time for a new Mob.*

Banji called up the dealership and ordered a Range Rover Sports. He agreed on a trade-in with his old SUV. He made payment later in the day, picked up his new grill and he was back at the ATMs in time for cashing in. This time, he was on the low about his new automobile. He was not throwing any wild party. He believed he was a grown man now.

***

Queen woke up to the first ray of sunlight that touched her closed eyes; it was 8.45 a.m. She started sneezing, her regular morning ritual. There was plenty of drinking in the clubs last night. She stretched her arms and yawned. She pulled the sheets off her body to the waist and sat with her back to the backrest of the bed; her beautiful tits clung firmly to her chest, and she looked like the sculpture of some Greek goddess.

The room was a white affair, furnished in good taste with expensive gadgets and fittings. A 42-inch TV hung on a corner wall, placed in a position that could be seen from the bed and the set of sofas. To the far left was a giant window, which served as the far left wall. It overlooked the Lagos lagoon. It was the Escalade Hotels, Lekki, rumored to be owned by some politician. A well-built masterpiece, it was smartly located on one of the best roads in Lagos. It was where the very big guys and game-players napped.

She was glad she got the chance to sleep in the hotel. Each time she traveled by, she wished to meet men that were paid enough to take her there; she and her friends had taken pictures of it about a year ago and now she lay in one of its beds.

She turned to look at the bad guy that had engaged her for the night, the heavy-set, dark-skinned, big-bellied, heavy snorer – a Matamba. She glowered with disappointment, staring angrily at the benumbed mass of flesh that lay in the same bed with her. As she was trying to get herself together, her phone began to ring. She got off the bed and turned around to see if the Matamba would wake up from the ringing. Cautiously, not wanting him to see the nudity he had played with heedlessly before they both passed out, she turned her head every two steps while tiptoeing to her bag that was almost falling off the sofa. She fetched her phone and silenced it before checking the caller ID. She turned to look again at the Matamba, who was still snoring into oblivion.

Satisfied that he wasn't going to wake up any moment soon, she took her time to wear her top and panties and then settled down to see to her phone.

"Oh, my God!" she exclaimed under her breath, seeing 22 missed calls from Ace. She moved from the call history to the idle screen of her phone to see the other communications she had missed. She had two text messages from Ace, several pings from him and her wonder friends, who chatted hustle gossip. Ace had pinged a lot of vexation and had cursed her in his text messages, mostly calling her "bitch."

The phone rang twice again; she decided not to take the call, taking her time to think of an excuse. Eventually, she went into the bathroom, having come up with what to say and placed a call through to Ace.

"What's his name?" Ace asked.

"What do you mean? You won't even say hello."

"I said what's his name, bitch?"

Queen ended the call at the mention of the word. She adjusted on the toilet seat, chuckling mischievously with a raised arm and whining in self-gratification. The phone rang again three times before she picked the call. "What?" she screamed into the phone, "What do you want?"

He cuts in, "Cool down..." paused for a second and said, "OK, tell me where you are."

"Am home."

"OK, why did it take you ages to pick my call? I've been calling you since Lord knows when."

"I've been sleeping."

"Are you coming around today?"

"Nope."

"Why?"

"Don't know."

"Fuck you, then."

"You, too."

They ended the madness after much cursing and arguing, and she went back into the room. She placed her phone on the ornamental center table, found the hotel directory, ordered breakfast, lit a cigarette and sat back to watch TV.

The phone rang once more.

"Hello."

"Ace, I have told you a million times never to call me bitch. Must I stab you for it to stick in your brain?" she said with the audacity she had trained herself with over her years of experience with men and their egos.

It was sort of working at that moment but, as usual, its potency was short-lived.

"I'm sorry, babes... I always tell you never to ignore my calls. You get me very worried when you do that, and besides I don't ever want you to leave my side... You're my soul, you know."

"Seen."

"So... what time am I seeing you today?"

"Not sure yet. Mom's not feeling so well, I have to attend to her. I'll call you soon as I can."

"Want me to come around?" Ace asked, sounding like a nice guy. "I think it's a good time to finally meet your mom."

"Ace, let's not talk about this for now. I'll let you know when the time is right... You know she still sees me as her little girl," she replied. She didn't allow guys to know where she was living but flaunted friends' houses as hers and always instructed men to park far off the street or wait at a particular landmark.

They talked a little longer and ended the conversation.

CHAPTER 3

In Benin, an ancient city with preserved traditions and customs, a land of history, occupied by warm and hospitable people, lived the Don… Grand Don as he was often called. The lanky five-foot-six, light-skinned, 34-year-old ex-soldier-turned-businessman loved his white dress code. He was always dressed in different forms of white; to him, the color white was symbolic of purity, honesty and plainness – so his late father told him. Son of a late voodoo priest, his father belonged to a clan of evildoers who were perceived as impeccant in the society. He grew up learning that the only way to survive was by wicked means under the pretext of benignity and benevolence. He learned sternness, cruelty and murder feigned in deceit from his only mentor and friend.

When he turned 14, his dad compelled him not to sleep until he got back home. He also asked him to keep the back door open and not the front. With blood on his hands and feet, he budged into the compound.

"Is everyone asleep?" his dad asked.

"Yes, Father," little Don replied.

"Good," Father said… "I have to talk to you, but first, get me some water and soap, I need to clean up."

"OK, Father."

The 58-year-old man tidied up and walked back into the house with the naïve teen. They sat in the quadrangle in the cool night breeze; females were not allowed in this perimeter of the house after ten o'clock. This time was reserved for the two men in the house. That particular night, there was a half-moon, giving some illumination and allowing them to see facial expressions clearly in the dark.

Father confessed murder to his only son for the first time. Although he had kept vigil since he was eight for his dad's occasional escapades, he'd always been blind to his compulsory vigil when others slept.

"Tonight, you will become a man. When I was about your age, your grandfather called me to this very spot and shared with me our family legacy." He paused for a moment and, putting a hand on Don's shoulder, shook him a bit, firmly, with the other hand. He raised his lean jaw and searched the depth of his eyes.

"You are fragile now but on the inside, you have the heart of the hyena… You will become a big-time scavenger and you will live on others' toiling. You will be hounded and ambushed but you will be like the breeze of the night, never to be caught.

"You will ease them and make them feel good," he stressed the 'good' to send a sensation to the little boy's enthusiastic spirit, "But you will make them sleep and you will take what belongs to them. They will hate you at night but will beseech you in the morning and they will worship you." With heavy barking and tensed tone, he said, "You will be a god!"

He performed a ritual from the materials he had prepared and spoke to him further on what happened that night and how he had made a living from murder and burglary. From that moment, little Nosa became peerless while he mastered the art of deceit and evil. He was fully-grown now; he joined the army at 19 and fought in a couple of battles, mostly in troubled regions of Africa. This act was a plot to earn him training in the use of firearms. He was in the artillery unit from day one; his ulterior motive, built around his unquantifiable enthusiasm, made him the best marksman in his battalion. He was a notorious sniper and a restless soldier.

Nosa was prolific at handling any rifle then and still was. He was a menacing weapon, a big threat to the law. He retired from the Army as a corporal at 25, travelled to Sweden and got married to a Swedish lady who bore him two daughters. He met some guys who were also in the hustle. He befriended them and was later introduced to some Indians and Pakistanis. A whole new world of crime was created in this camp. They exposed him to some new levels of making good money, a whole new perspective, different from what he had always known. He had sleepless nights over the choice of vocation he would stick to. He concluded there was no harm making the dough from different avenues; after all, everyone spoke about having multiple streams of income.

While in the army, he had mixed up with men of the underworld, men like wolves, fearless and witty. They liked the ease with which he related with them, especially for someone who was in law enforcement. He earned good loot from two outings, which was enough for him to travel out of the country. Now he was all grown, vast and very experienced in the get-rich-or-die-trying world.

He had left the armed robbery game to the boys, but they still sought him for inspiration and advice from time to time. Now he was A-class in the 419 business-owning houses in some major cities around the world. A venture capitalist, he was involved financially in a couple of companies that did real well, and his achievements had turned him into the spirit-like being his father prayed he would become. A brute and inconsiderate human being, he was very dreaded, as his common statement was *"An eye for an eye."* He was the whole nine yards at crazy stuff; his animal instincts made him a predominant rapist.

***

"Guy, I'll offer you 30 percent. There's a long list that's yet to be executed. If your client is really rich, we can fix your job at number five. Ask around, dude, I don't talk much," Don said, boasting.

"Bros, make it 60 – 40 please," the voice at the other end replied, pleading.

Don ended the call abruptly and put his phone away.

"These small boys believe it's easy to get things done, if only they knew what it took me to get to where I am today, they'd accord me with maximum respect. None of you should ever introduce me to cock-suckers like that again, else I'll treat all your fuck-ups!"

In the patio of his exquisite mansion, a couple of men in their twenties sat to listen to Don's instructions while some were shooting pool. Elegantly furnished with state-of-the-art gadgets and Italian and Persian furniture, it was a ten-bedroom house with three living rooms, a big conference/dining room, a den, one big kitchen with two smaller ones, two patios and more. A smart architectural expression of the capital letter D, the perimeter within the arch was mostly covered by a big swimming pool with an artificial waterfall positioned to the west of it where sunlight hit the most. The long straight line of the letter D was a massive barbed wire fence that demarcated the pool end of the house from the basketball and tennis courts.

The house was strategically built on a 10-acre hilltop; Don liked the feeling of sitting on top of the world. It was five minutes of driving from the house's main gate to the nearest community. Unwelcome visitors and hikers dreaded going near the house. Rumor had it that a special breed of wild Australian dogs guarded the house. This particular breed was a nightmare to kangaroos in their nativity and they were feared to relish the taste of human blood.

There were two apartment buildings towards the southeast end of the house. They were a story each of 15 small rooms, which could be better described as a dormitory. Every room was en-suite with a little kitchen designed for workers and the boys. One of these two buildings was fully occupied by boys. Each room was equipped with a 32-inch LED TV, a home theater system, a 6-by-6-feet bed, a sofa, small fridge, desk and chair – and of course an iMac and a Windows laptop, all connected to the house server via Wi-Fi.

The boys were the bloodstream of the organization. They slept and woke on the computer. Their primary assignment was to continually send spam emails in millions every day. Every potential client's file was passed through departments in stages of complexity and prospect.

Don had a dream of ruling the country someday; this made him think ahead and plan his ways. It also kept him organized and cultured in the running of his empire. The boys were sold the vision, too; that kept them well behaved and comported while they religiously lived by the facade of working with Don as staff and managers of his portfolio. They were not boys from this state. Whenever they went out to town, they were perceived as expatriates. All drove brand-new official cars with the insignia "Metro Investments."

"Vitali!" Don summoned the 28-year-old Russian. "You are seating a job in Italy. You will fly there tonight. Stanley will pick you at the airport and show you around town." He stood up from where he was seated and walked towards Vitali; his skinny frame was about a quarter the size of this Russian macho – a big contrast between boss and subordinate. He looked at him sarcastically and beckoned him to follow his stroll as he made his way toward the sunny poolside.

This British-born Russian had met the little Don four years ago while trying to pick his pocket at a train station in Liverpool. He met his match that day. His hand was caught in a reflex action and was brought down to his knees with a broken finger. Don stared him in the eyes and immediately found loyalty in the sober lad; he saw potential, too. Realizing the act was about to be blown in the air, with the broken finger Don dragged him to the nearest toilet; luckily it was only 15 feet away.

"Never steal from a black man again in your life!" Little Don said, bawling.

"Take these 200 pounds." He fetched 10 crisp 20-pound notes from a stack of 80 neatly kept in an inner pocket of his high fashion leather jacket. "Get yourself laid tonight, and when you get a clear head in the morning, gimme a call at this number." He scribbled some digits on a piece of paper he tore from a poster. He tapped him on the back and said to him, "Be a good boy, and I'll make you rich."

Don left him staring in awe. He got home and kept the paper in his Bible, then threw a little crack party with two friends all night. He didn't call until he got out of jail eight months later for stealing an old lady's bag. Jail hadn't meant much to him in the past, but this time, he wasn't going back for petty crime. He cried several nights. His cellmate was the boss of a jail gang. He was handpicked for the boss on his entry into jail and was forcefully lured into sex. Luckily, Don was in Spain when he called; glad to hear from him, he was sent an e-ticket two days later.

For the first time in his life, he slept in a five-star hotel, and it was for a stretch of four days. He was introduced to some big boys and was schooled on Don's kind of racket. It was entirely new to him but seemed pretty cool. For another nine months, he went through different trainings on Internet scams and ended up blending easily into phishing. He got tools freely from an online machine where spammers met to trade tools. He became successful at this because he could relate easily with his Russian counterparts, who were known to be hacking kings, and also hackers from different countries around the world. He never defaulted on payment of cuts, as Don mandated he kept his integrity with people he worked with. It was Don's personal policy to keep to his word in business, as he usually said, "The thief with integrity rules the gang and always gets external jobs begging for his attention."

There were times Don made him pay consolatory monies to his hackers on event of failed jobs. He became a cash cow for Don as he opened a whole new moneymaking venture for him. Don soon became the kingpin in banking fraud. He only got involved in large sums. The minimum he would do was 100,000, and he wouldn't touch any currency other than pounds, euros or dollars. There was a time they got lucky with an account of eight million pounds, and they moved 750,000 from it twice. He was on a steady cash-in of 40 to 50 percent, 10 percent to the hacker or Vitali, 10 percent to the middleman and 30 percent to the cash-out (account owner). Vitali always got 10 percent. Although he grumbled a couple of times, he was only staff and he owed all loyalty to the boss. Without him, he'd still be on the streets hustling petty crime.

He would liaise with the other boys who worked for Don to make some fast cash for themselves. They usually did crumbs. The boys chatted up their friends on Yahoo messenger, collated account details of clients and made bank transfers on their behalf. This was usually not a sure venture, but the few coins that materialized were good to throw around at the clubs. Only Don had the connection for sure money. He usually got word on the bits but never raised an eyebrow. The amounts were too small for him to bother.

Meanwhile, Vitali was being coached on the main business the boss was into; being Caucasian gave him a whole lot of edge over everybody else. His splendid use of English and the British accent gave him a lot of leverage and made work go very smoothly, as he was always considered to be real. There was no arrangement he was involved in that flopped. He handled most of the calls and, at some point, he brought in a fellow junkie, "Sophie," a British-born Croatian.

Sophie was a plus-size 22-year-old. Blonde, green eyes, five-foot-nine and 90kg. She was very cuddly, but lonely in her soul. She was always in need of a guy around. She regularly craved sex and made advances to every guy she desired. She was of the belief that her plus size was a minus for her, so rather than wait for a guy to make a move, she was up in your face asking if you'd share her bed.

She was endowed with large tits but unfortunately had a very flat behind and a protruding tummy. Her teeth were milky brown from smoking too many cigarettes, weed and having an unhealthy lifestyle. She did a good job, although it took some training to blend into the system. She never left the house because she had a loose mouth; if she had to go out for any reason, she was subjected to close monitoring or escorted.

Because of the restriction and her not-so-good looks, she flirted with the workers in the house, and they took turns sharing her bed. It was heaven for her here, though; she got all the sex she wanted, all the weed in the world and plenty of sunlight, plus a swimming pool. What does she care about money? Nada. She was not bothered as long as she had a steady supply of her daily needs. It only made sense for the outfit to claim they were situated in the U.K. They had plenty of roamed British SIM cards, three satellite phones, various websites with London office addresses and, of course, two Britons to convince anybody in the world how legitimate their operations were.

"This is a difficult one, Vitali, and I hate that you're the one to execute it."

Vitali stiffened as Don declared the solemn words. "You're very experienced, and I know you'll deliver. I'm sure the mugu *(fool)* will buy it big time as you're Caucasian. The reason for the fear is that he is an ex-general and is known to be very tactful. He's very rich – if the job is done well, we can milk him of 20 million or more. His house is heavily guarded, and he always carries a gun. You'll be seeing a dentist in Lagos when we touch down. Your prey is very keen on hygiene. He's a tidy freak. Stanley has a pair of well-polished, fairly used brogues and an 85-oyster date, just waiting for you. He will respect you dressed in these. Wear a black jacket, a pair of brown khakis and white polo. Be calm all through and choose your words carefully… you'll be fine."

"Sure, boss, I'll handle him fine…I know his type," Vitali replied assuredly. He had read many crime novels and seen loads of mafia movies.

"Atta boy!"

"Yes boss… I got this one." He got up from the pool bench he sat on beside Don and walked away.

Somewhere in Italy, in a little town bed and breakfast, bald-headed Stanley got busy preparing stuff for Vitali's job. He shopped for an HP laser jet printer, different colors of pens, some paper that varied in sizes, color and thickness, a board and cutter, stamp ink, a dozen hard rectangular soaps and more.

Stanley took the room in the pretext of a freelance writer. He did that to cover up for the delivery of the printer and all the paperwork he had to do. The 52-year-old fat guy was a veteran con artist. He had been in the game since the days of the manual typewriters. Back then, the grind was done mostly hardware, and learning the job required a two-year apprenticeship. Printing was tedious; there were no computers and personal printers. In his time, they were comfortable with small money. The most he made was $20,000, but hits were regular. His peers were contented with little money. They were rich men back home and they often threw big parties. Most of them went broke and now did menial jobs to survive. Fat Stanley got lucky only for being distant cousins with Don. The boss picked him up and dusted him off after serving 12 years in a New Jersey jail for drug peddling. Don recruited him for his printing skills and his wide travels. He was totally loyal to the Don and earned a good living working for him.

He fabricated very authentic-looking documents from the paper he had bought. He already had the formats to the documents on his Apple laptop; all he did per time was to edit names, location and dates. He cut clean moulds on the soap bars, dusted them off with a soft makeup brush and created perfect impressions of company seals. Stanley also prepared every other thing needed for the job, everything to the letter. The boss never took chances at anything; he liked to be like God by creating the destiny of every single job he undertook. For this to come to realization, he oversaw everything from the accent used in conversations to the way your boxers were worn. He also kept vigil and prayed fervently for success. He was a devout Christian but evil in his dealings. He was also an ordained deacon at a local Pentecostal church, where he worshipped and donated a handful of money to the propagation of the gospel.

CHAPTER 4

The black Range Rover pulled up at the parking lot of the Muritala Muhammed Airport, Lagos. Young Banji paced briskly towards the arrival end. He was 36 minutes late, but things don't happen on time anyway. He was right on time – Bros was just about calling.

"Hey little man, how've you been?"

"I've been good, boss. I miss you, sir!"

Bros tapped him at the back of his head; he turned around and took up a boxing position. Bros did the same, and they sparred for a second in the presence of a laughing crowd.

"You think I'll grow too old to fall you? I got game always!"

They talked at length while they walked to the SUV.

"You're doing pretty good, young man. I admire your courage for getting a VOGUE. It must be the best ride in your school."

"Bros, I top the league in anything I do!"

"That's my boy. I see you making a lot of money off me, eh. Anyway, you got work to do. You're heading for Algeria tomorrow…"

Banji cut in, "But I got exams for the next three days."

"Fuck exams, Banj, you got work to do."

"OK, boss, you know I love to work. I smell some big brew in the mill!"

Bros picked up his telephone and began a long conference call. Banji concentrated on the road and drove to Blue Isle Hotel Maryland, a South African bed and breakfast.

"When was this built? Looks really nice…" Bros looked around in bewilderment. "Is this where you live now?"

"Naa, boss, you need somewhere quiet and discrete… This is the best I could find for the best Bros in the world," Banji answered with a grin.

"My boy sure knows good stuff." Bros continued his phone conversation. Banji fetched his single piece of luggage; Bros usually travelled light. He followed Banji's lead and ended the call on the flight of stairs. His room was 101, the Presidential.

"Voila!" little Banji exclaimed soon, as Bros saw what awaited him in the luxury room.

"Banj Banj, now you've gone really bad!"

Banji introduced Bros to the three beautiful ladies who welcomed the big man. The party had already begun. Two bottles of Rosé were almost empty, and there was loud Naija music, too. The hotel room was a large one with a king-sized bed in the middle, tastefully furnished with two giant African paintings and a sculpture neatly arranged at different sides of the room.

"Good to meet you, cuties. You will have to gimme a second to freshen up; this tired old piece of relic needs a good shower, and it's been a long flight, you know."

Banji asked to be excused to sort something in town. Bros stepped into the inviting Jacuzzi; he wasn't fully settled in the warm lather when the slim frame of a model slipped into the bath unannounced. The ménage à quatre began.

Banji returned three hours later but met no response to his repeated raps on the door. He called room service to open it with a spare key and encountered the four all passed out in bed. He helped himself to some drink while the tired folks woke up one after the other, picking up their clothing in nudity and not caring about the unacquainted accomplice. Bros was last to get up; seeing Banji, he exclaimed sleepily, "Bad boy, very bad boy... I'm gonna have to keep you at arm's length, crazy little thing."

Banji chuckled, feeling good with himself. He had a six-pack and usually dressed in different colors of singlet, sagged jeans, baseball caps and mostly white sneakers. He was a lover of bling, too, brandishing different sizes of necklaces and oversized wristwatches.

"Boss, how's it going?" He walked toward the liquor table and poured himself another stiff X.O. "Is there anything you need? Just say the word."

"I'm OK for now; I'm in good hands, as you can see. We'll be going out later tonight to discuss business."

"OK, boss, enjoy. I'm in the next room – holla when you need me."

"Sure, little man."

He left to his room, where some really beautiful lady awaited him.

***

In the chauffeur-driven Bentley, with the three beauties dressed aggressively sexy, he arrived at Club Football. Bros liked to make a statement anywhere he went. Banji drove behind in his Range. He was with Ace, the girl from his room and another girl he arranged for Ace. They were met by greeters who opened the doors and ushered them in. Banji's truck was driven after Bros's car to be parked by a valet.

There was uniqueness in the club's treatment of the A-class; two bouncers were attached to the super-rich from the entrance. They were led to the VVIP section. The three tall cuties holding hands with Bros, Banji and Ace followed with their girls beside them. The club was owned by a footballer. It was converted from an old massive warehouse. This provided enough space to create a football pitch replica. The VIP and VVIP sections were positioned at the far ends meant for goal posts. Both were covered in tinted glass from floor to ceiling. These sections were two floors each. They were decorated with jerseys of soccer stars, autographed footballs and other memorabilia displayed in secured cases and glass.

The VIP area was open to anyone but subject to the discretion of its greeter, while the VVIP section only admitted select guests. It was believed that legislators and top government officials discreetly hung out there. A private passageway through the back door led to a secure enclosure where highly classified meetings were hosted. That was where the gods in government and the underworld determined the fate of a chunk of the economy.

The supposed pitch was stylishly furnished with multicolored couches and varieties of stools and abstract sitting objects. There was a giant bar on one side, stretching 60 feet. It catered for every drink you could think of. Some Hungarians were shocked to find their traditional vodka.

"It's hard to believe they are exported," they announced. On the other end was a massive stage. It was the best clubbing experience anywhere. Don got to his feet to welcome Bros. They hugged, shook hands and introduced their entourages. The picture of Don hugging Bros showed how little the rich thug was. They all settled into the comfortable furniture as more champagne was brought in. They discussed shallow issues and did the regular gossip of current happenings around the world, politics and girls.

Some 20 minutes into the acquaintances, Don and Bros picked up their glasses and walked to a separate sofa.

"What's up little man, everything working to plan?"

"Yea, big man, the kid is on the plane already."

"Good, your fat guy on standby?"

"Everything is perfect from my end. I should be asking about yours."

"Trust me… my little nephew will see to Algeria. He'll set out in the morning."

"Correct, I can milk this guy of 20 million… he's loaded."

"Don Don! I admire your optimism, but then you're a veteran, I'll never doubt your competence. There's a handful of boys waiting on your expertise in London, but man, you're too choosy. Cut these boys some slack – they worship you."

"Bambi, you know I have to be careful at this job. I take my time when choosing clients. I got a reputation to keep as a responsible citizen and legit businessman, you know," he replied humorously.

"Bad guy!" Bros said and chuckled. They shook hands and laughed extensively at cheap talk. "I should introduce my nephew to you." He called Banji to join them.

"You know the Don, right? You'll be meeting him more often from now."

Banji bowed a little to acknowledge him with respect. "I've heard a lot about you, boss! You're a legend! Wanna be like you when I grow up!"

"Banj Banj, heard about you, too – and your wits… Don't worry, you'll get there; the young usually grow into better masters, especially with the right mentorship. Be free to come by the house anytime. You should meet my boys."

"Can't wait, boss, heard a lot about the castle – must be heaven!"

"Big Banji, funny lil Banji." The two older men liked the kid. They called him different funny names.

They discussed business for some three minutes and headed back to the party. Ace was already dancing sensually with his girl, holding her by the hip and moving to the urban reggae music in the air. She was holding him on the head with her back to him; Banji bumped in to take his place. Banji got the party started as the D.J. played a brand new Naija hit almost immediately. Most of the pack got up to the flow. Ace decided to see what the popular side felt like and probably get some weed. He waded through the cranked-up crowd; it was a Friday night, the new club was filled to its brim. He eventually made his way outside the club to some peace and quiet. He talked to one of the bouncers who pointed to the weed guy. He got hooked up with some laced weed, smoked a joint at the corner and kept the remaining to offer to anyone who'd be interested. On his way back, he chatted up two horny girls about to make out; they laughed to his little joke and exchanged BlackBerry pins. *You never know when they'll come in handy*, he told himself. They talked about having a private party in his apartment sometime, and then he walked back to the VVIP feeling like a player.

Ace joined the groove and told Banji he'd gotten weed. Banji announced: A couple of them scrambled for some; others ignored and continued in status quo. Ace picked up his glass, sipped some champagne and sat beside Bros. They chatted over unimportant stuff when Banji suddenly asked if Ace invited Queen to the club.

Almighty Don and Majestic Queen, Ace thought to himself. He lost it when he saw them but, advised otherwise by Bros, he laid back. She was pinned to the wall and touched all over. The sight of his woman in the hands of the little freak gave this fun-loving lad the biggest daze of his life. She was having fun, obviously; the jest was real.

"I need to cool off, Ace, had so much fun the past days. Go seal the deal and bring money home to mama," she had told him.

CHAPTER 5

Somewhere in Algeria, Mahmud, 22, returned home from the shops carrying two big bags of groceries. He had installed new air conditioning in the spare room the previous day. A devout Muslim, he put away the stuff and knelt by his mat to pray. Mahmud sat at his table, worried about what to feed his anticipated guest; he did a little research on Nigerian food. Having heard a lot about Nigeria and its various tribes, he went straight to search for Yoruba food and possible online cookbooks. He found a handful of info and smiled.

He was an aspiring chef and a very good cook. He learned the mastery of good cooking from his mom. She was one of the best cooks around; she led the cooking team at major festivals and Ramadan. She was well known for her special pudding and couscous. She was loved by her late husband, who died when their son was only five years old. Mahmud grew into a fine young man, obedient and intelligent. He'd been classified a genius from elementary school and had fallen in love with computers in secondary school. He was discovered by an older boy in school who mentored him on hacking.

Initially, his activities were primarily to hack the school database to prove he was good, Internet servers for free usage, fight mafia wars and other petty stuff, until he met some Scandinavian on a Yahoo messenger chat room. This stranger developed some liking to him and taught him everything in the world of hacking in return for recruiting an army of younger hackers. Since then, he had been a hacker to reckon with. His alliance with fraudsters opened his eyes to moneymaking. His initial mentor banned him from his group and had since become an enemy. He also had a big flair for Forex trading; he'd gambled a lot of his early earnings to it until he became really good. Now he traded big time and invested virtually all he earned in the New York Stock Exchange, although Mama still saw him as her cute little grown man who's simply in love with computers.

He was really anticipating the coming of his Internet best friend. They'd known each other for a while and had done a lot together. Getting to meet in real life was quite fascinating, and he sure wanted to give his friend a befitting treat. The job was not as important to him as meeting an online business partner and bud. He picked up his phone and sent an SMS: "I'm ready for you."

***

6.45 next morning, Vitali walked briskly through the crowd, exiting at the arrival end of the Malpensa Airport. Spotting Stanley, he wore a big grin, tapped his bald head and kissed it. Stanley hit him lightly in the tummy… their way of saying hello.

"Wetin dey, Fatso *(What's up, fatso)*?"

"I dey long *(I'm OK)*, idiot."

"How's the little man?"

"Hostile!"

"Who upset him this time?"

"Nobody," he shrugged and turned pale. "How would he have me do this job? This guy I'm meeting is a psycho with a gun. I'd hate to die in Italy – would prefer Naija." He braced up as he continued, "Let's go make some Euros!"

Stanley giggled, knowing the hunk was weak-willed but always delivered. They walked to the small rented Fiat and drove to the bed and breakfast. Stanley filled him in on the job. They also talked at length about the Don; they laughed hysterically about his quirky ways as they drove into the Milan hills.

***

Banji's phone rang the third time. Reluctantly, he woke up, swearing; as soon as he saw the caller ID, he abruptly came to life.

"Shit, I'm late!" he exclaimed as he checked the time on his watch. He still had his giant necklace and other jewels on him. It was 7.30 a.m., and his flight was scheduled for 8.55. He picked the call and…

"What's wrong with you?" the voice at the other end screamed.

"Good morning, sir." He hit himself on the head, struggling to sound serious and to conceal his chuckle.

"Will you shut up and get your ass out of bed; I want you in that airport in two minutes!"

"Yes, boss!"

He got up, squeezing his way through the half-dead nude bodies. "I'm the bad guy," he said to himself as he looked at the four naked girls. He kicked Ace in the back to wake him up. "Wake up, dude, we're late!"

"Late for what?"

"Forgetful idiot! Algeria, duhh!"

As he walked toward the bathroom at the far end of the room, he looked at the girl cuddled in a couch all dressed up and laughed. "You didn't sleep, right? Sure you enjoyed the live adult movie hehehe."

She stuck out her tongue annoyingly. "Bad boy," she called him and turned her head away from naked Banji. She hadn't joined the spree. She liked to party but didn't do the sex. Her friends made jest of her always and called her names. She ignored them but still kept them. She was a good girl, they said, had two rape incidents but survived both untouched. She knew how to escape hurt. The two girls making out when Ace got weed had pinged him that they needed a ride. They had warned him of their friend; he wasn't bothered anyway. Two were a handful; besides, he was with a girl already. He had to get the Queen-Don episode off his mind quickly.

Banji was out of the bathroom in two minutes. Ace jumped in and was out before Banji got dressed. There was no time to get the change of clothing. Banji's box and Ace's change of clothing were left in the SUV. The girls were now awake.

"Sorry, girls, we'll have to leave you now. I'm late for my flight. We'll keep in touch." He brought out his wallet, took out five $100 bills and some naira; he dropped the cash on the bed.

"You guys will find your way around easily – call the reception and they'll arrange a cab for you. Ciao." Ace also said goodbye, walked to the girl who didn't play and pecked her on the forehead.

"You're my kinda girl. Have my phone. I'll call you on it."

She was flabbergasted.

The two boys raced to Bros's room and rapped on the door. The door was opened by one of the girls, wrapped in sheets. They rushed in and made respectful gestures facetiously.

"Sorry, boss!" they both apologized solemnly.

"I'll skin the two of you if you miss that flight and I'll make you go through the desert to Mahmud. Get going before I lose my mind!"

On their way, Ace snatched Banji's phone and put a call through to his phone.

"Hello," she said.

"Babes, I'll call you before noon. Don't pick up any calls, OK? When you receive two beeps of the same number, the third being a full ring, that'll be me. Talk to you soon." He hung up and returned the phone.

"Guy, now I know you're nuts. What if you don't get your phone back... have you considered never seeing her again? All the stuff on your phone – what if she goes through them or picks up a call from one of your magas *(clients)*?"

"She won't."

"It's your phone, do what you want with it."

They arrived at the airport in nine minutes. Banji got out at the departure while Ace parked the car. He walked back to the departure to meet Banji checking his bag in.

"Almost missed the check-in, man."

"Lucky bastard!"

"Got to board now. Be set for your part, OK?"

"Go easy on them Arab girls."

They both laughed and hugged. Banji departed.

***

Ace pulled up at his regular parking lot: a mall, four streets away from his home. His parents had no knowledge of him owning a car. The two security guys on duty raced to meet him as he opened the door.

"Oga *(Boss)*, Baba God don do am *(God has done it)*. You don hammer *(You've hit it big)*!" They saluted and made respectful gestures. Ace smiled and gave them a thousand naira to share.

"I'll be back in three hours," he told them and left. He walked to a retail store and bought a CDMA hand phone. He did as he told her, and she picked the call.

"Hey beautiful."

"Hey."

They talked at length; he pleaded with her to understand that what happened through the night was a result of hurt and that he was not the type to do a couple of girls and all. He explained he had just suffered heartbreak, that he'd liked her the moment he saw her but thought she was like her other friends. He said the fact that she didn't indulge in the fling proved she was different. He told her he was high and the group stuff was too tempting to be resisted. On and on he went, until she said to stop.

"When and where are you picking up your phone?"

"I have to see my mom for two hours; I will call you as soon as I'm done."

"What were you thinking, leaving your phone with a stranger? Are you insane? It's a Bold 6 for crying out loud. My friends are forcing me to sell it!"

"You wouldn't do that, I know. I trusted you from the start."

"Anyway, your phone has been ringing all morning, had to plug it in so I wouldn't miss your call."

Hearing this, Ace made a victory gesture, feeling good about her caring.

"Thanks a lot, sweetheart," he said calmly, not wanting her to notice his flush.

"Don't thank me, I'm just being upright. I've never taken what doesn't belong to me."

"Thanks all the way. I will holla at you when I'm done with Mom's."

He hung up and boarded an okada *(commercial motorcycle)*. Ace came from a modest household. Both parents were respectable civil servants. They have worked dutifully and honorably all their life. They have been good parents, too. His mom would probably collapse at the knowledge that he owned a car and would perhaps go into coma if she knew he'd built a house of his own.

He still received weekly stipends and returned home fortnightly. Each time he didn't get a bank alert, he knew his folks were playing a con to lure him home when they missed him. He loved his parents so much but hardly spent a night at home. He was a grown man now and could fend for himself beyond expectation.

"Mom, hope we're not out for long. I have to prepare for tomorrow's test."

"Dayo, I know it when you lie, you naughty boy… Don't worry, we'll be on time. I know you like to be with your friends always."

They got into his mother's 2006 Toyota Corolla and they headed for her brother's house. She asked him to pull over at a big car mart, telling him she needed to see someone there. She stopped by a 2004 Honda Accord and asked if he liked the car.

"It's not bad, Ma, but it's too small for you. Told you to get yourself a C-class – that's what suits you."

"Funny boy, I'm buying it for you. It's just N1.5 million, it's got leather and comes with full options, just as you've always wanted, your dream car."

The moment boggled him, and his heart skipped two beats.

"Mom, you're kidding. Why are you buying me a car? It's not my graduation or my birthday. Besides, you guys have got loads of obligations."

"Not to worry Dayo, we love you and want the best for you. Your dad just got promoted to permanent secretary; we decided to surprise you with this."

He wore a wide grin; he couldn't hide the joy anymore. He hugged her tightly and pecked her on the cheek.

"Thank you, Mom. I really appreciate this, but you know what? There's this 2001 Honda that a friend offered me. It's very nice and in perfect shape. He wants to sell at N500,000. We can save one million if we buy that one. Remember, I'm still a student."

"Forget it. It's been paid for already. We know the type of cars boys your age use these days and we see your friends' cars when they come home with you. We don't want something too small for you."

Confused but madly happy, he grabbed his mom again and pecked her all over. He then prostrated to show respect and appreciation.

"Get up, silly boy. Why embarrass yourself in public?"

He got up and hugged her more. "Thank you, Ma," he kept saying.

"Your dad is in Abuja, you don't need to sleep home to thank him. Call him on the phone. Call your brother, too – he contributed 500,000. He's been in Calabar for two days; he loved the idea of you having a car and sent his contribution immediately."

"I will, I will," he said, still very surprised.

"Here's N50,000, you may want to take your friends out today," she said as she fetched a bale of N500 notes, "Buy Queen a little surprise, too, and tell her I miss her. I've not spoken to her in a while, I've been very busy. Want to see her soon!"

The mention of the name brought a sour taste to his mouth and changed his mood, but he made sure he didn't show it.

"I will, Ma," he said subtly.

They obtained all the papers to the car, and she released him. "We don't have to go home together. Go to school and have fun," she insisted, and they parted ways.

***

Some minutes after noon, at the Houari Boumediene Airport Algiers, Banji walked in his usual hip strides, feeling like a hip-hop star, out to the waiting locals and cab men. Mahmud was right there, carrying a placard with the inscription "BANJ BANJ" written conspicuously. He had seen several pictures of Banji and recognized him immediately. He shouted his name a couple of times, but Banji ignored him. He walked up to him, tapping him on the shoulder.

"Mr Banj, I am Mahmud, your friend, online, we do business. I expect you, I am good cook. Don't let me talk too much; you disgrace me in front of my brethren please," the French-speaking Arab pleaded.

Banji looked at him sarcastically and walked away screaming, "Kidnapper I don't know you!"

Poor Mahmud folded himself in shame and squeezed his cardboard. He walked away in disbelief.

"Banj will call me when he needs me," he told himself. As he walked away in disappointment, Banji began to gag, calling "Aboki! *(Friend!)* Mahmud! Come back here! You fell for the simple tease too easily," Banji said. "Let's go home to eat your food."

The crowd laughed at the little drama. Mahmud walked back to him, happy that he'd been acknowledged. He was a shy guy, he detested embarrassment. With his feminine voice he said, "You are bad man, Banj."

They shook hands, and Banji dragged him into a big hug. "It's really cool to meet you finally, man!" he said. They both laughed and walked to Mahmud's car.

***

Ace met Ella at an agreed eatery; he had missed a couple of calls and had a number of texts and BlackBerry messages, too – a lot from Queen and some international calls.

"Your girlfriend called several times. It's obvious she's a Queen," she giggled.

"Forget her; she's no longer the one for me. Can't stand her anymore, I've had it to the lid," he replied with a face.

"Seen." She changed position and locked her eyes on Ace. "What do you do for a living?"

"School."

"Hmm, that makes you receive this many international and unknown calls?" She stretched across the table and reached for his shirt collar. "Dude, I don't do yahoo boys, OK?"

"What do you mean by that?"

"You heard me right, and I'm sure you know what I mean. I need to tell you about me... I'm not what you're looking for. I may seem like most other girls, crazy and all, but man, I'm not your regular girl."

"I know that, and please – I'm no yahoo boy," he answered. "Anyway, let's not go there. I know you're different and I want to be a friend. I can see all over you that I can trust you. Let's not rush things. Let's keep it simple and see where this leads, capisce?"

"Capisce."

They talked regular talk and caught up on things. They also savored some light Naija music in the background.

"Can I be honored with your digits, ma'am?"

"Well of course, sir, you've been a gentleman so far."

"Can I also take you home?" he asked, not expecting a positive response.

"It's down the street, but it's OK. You can save me a little walk."

He drove her to her home, hugged her, saw she got into her house and drove off.

***

They drove two hours from the airport to Bouga. Mahmud helped Banji with his bag as they climbed the flight of stairs. They were met by his mom, who welcomed Banji warmly.

"You look like little bow bow," she said. "And you eat well, Mahmud," she shook her head disapprovingly. "He don't like food… he thin, very thin." She touched him on the head and then carried his big pendant. "You good boy, eat well, big weight and you rich… very rich."

They all laughed.

"I'm a good boy, ma'am," Bow Wow said.

"Ma is cook good couscous for you, you enjoy it."

He gesticulated and rubbed his tummy, "I want all the couscous right now, this dawg is hungry!"

"You is no dog, you is a man, strong man!" she bragged, clenching her fists to show strength. Mahmud cut in, speaking Arabic, and told his mom the guy needed to rest and do some catching up. He dragged his friend deeper into the house and showed him to the guest room.

"Ma can talk all day if you give her a chance."

"I can talk all month, man. I like your mom; she's just like my mom. She always wants you fed."

Mahmud showed him around the house and eventually his own room.

"Damn, you've got more computers than NASA, man!" he exclaimed at the sight of the four large monitors on the Arab guy's desk. "You must have access to the World Bank's database with these gigantic computers, really… you kidding me?"

"This is not much my friend; it is what I do with it that's important. All these you see are heavy-duty workstations with incredible memory and processing speed. I have direct connection with a satellite in space and I am my own server. I also have a whole desktop as VPN, which self-destructs at any tracking within a 50-kilometer radius of this place. I can't afford to buy a new computer every day, meaning my VPN is very strong," he dragged the word strong. Banji smiled with approval; he was super-impressed.

"I have access to the latest United States secret weapon. I really love it, but it's for my consumption only." He showed his tongue to tease his visitor. "There's no new hacking tool I don't have, and I compete with the best hackers in the world in wars to stamp my feet as a master. I am training plenty more around the world. It's great fun. I sit by my computer for weeks without seeing sunlight. Ma complains all the time, but I lock my door. She doesn't complain anymore – she's used to it. I will show you plenty of things before you go, but first let us have lunch. Ma must be waiting to feed you. You are her new son," he giggled. "After food, I take you club and buy you Rozay."

Banji laughed, "Rozay? In this desert?"

"We have Nuvo, Ciroc, all the drinks in hip-hop videos. Owner of the club often travels to the USA and he brings all the hip things from there. We have Cuban cigars, too."

"Well, I'm astonished," he said with a dropped jaw. "Until I see, though…"

"Let's go eat, brother."

They fed on a tray of couscous and talked at length enjoying Naija stories.

CHAPTER 6

At the white villa of General Wikki, he pressed twice on the buzzer at the gate. A voice on the other side asked in Italian who it was, and he responded by mentioning his first name. The gate opened and closed after him. He strolled up the porch to the main door of the house. A lover of flowers and a landscape artisan, he ignored the beautiful plants that he would have savored on a good day. With his heart in his mouth and his bladder about to burst, he summoned all the courage he could muster and calculated his every step.

I'd rather be in Don's house sipping on liquor and smoking a big blunt than be on this job right now, he thought to himself. He had been scared since the first mention of the job and, now that he was in the premises of the dreaded war veteran, he wished he could turn back. He was met by a lady dressed in an apron; he perceived her to be a badass soldier disguised as a maid. He frisked her with his eyes, suspecting she might be carrying a gun. She made some gestures and said hallo, the only word she said. This scared him more, forgetting he wasn't in an English-speaking country. She led him through the beautiful three-centuries-old mansion to a gigantic dual door, each one twice his height. He couldn't stop looking around through the corners of his eyes but maintained composure.

The door revealed a medium-sized hall surrounded with shelves of very old books – more books than his high school library had. At the big window on the far end sat the general, who he presumed was half as old as the desk and the desk half as old as the house. Unmoved by the presence of the visitor, the square-faced old-timer scared him to death. The maid left and shut the door behind her; he walked towards the mute scary old man. As he got closer, the evil-looking host picked up the 1934 Beretta that lay in front of him, cocked it and pointed it at Vitali. He pulled the trigger almost immediately. Vitali collapsed to the floor at the sound of the click.

"Wake up, young man." The old man tapped him on the face and helped him up. He laughed hysterically as he lifted the big man to his feet. "I got you on that one!" he said. Vitali felt like a child, embarrassed and confused. Unsure of his safety, he braced himself and decided to await the worst that could happen in calmness.

"It's an old joke that was played on me when I was captain; I planned on doing the same since then but had not found who to play with. Mi dispiace *(I'm sorry)*. I'm Alexandra Wikki; you're James Branden, I believe."

"Yes, I am," he managed to muscle out of his now-heavy mouth.

"I've done a lot of research on you and your partners – you guys have got pretty impressive records." He walked around the table to his antique chair and asked Vitali to take a seat.

"Espresso or cappuccino?"

Feeling a little easier, he realized his guts had dried out of exhaustion and fear and hurriedly asked for espresso. Don had instructed him on the choice of coffee.

"Haven't had a good laugh in ages... Thanks for coming. I'll adopt you as my son if you'll visit me every month," he chuckled.

In your dreams, Vitali thought to himself.

"Don't know why I have this sudden liking for you, kid. You remind me of my best friend who died in the war – great man, he died a martyr."

They chatted for several minutes about war; luckily, Vitali's mother was a soldier before he was born. She often fed him with tales of war and intelligence; it influenced his quest for war knowledge. The retired general was impressed by the broadness of his knowledge. He liked him more. They moved from coffee to vodka, from desk to sofa and soon they both became like boys talking and laughing about girls, cars, teachers in high school and more.

Suddenly remembering his reason for being there after two hours of merriment, he jumped back to reality and asked the general if they could proceed to the business he came for.

"Shut up and drink, lad. I have your check ready. I don't get this much attention at my old age."

Overcome with amazement, Vitali sighed some relief, although inconspicuously. He was wary of being taken for a ride. He coughed, excused himself and got to his feet as he proceeded to his laptop bag. The old man walked ahead to his chair and pulled a drawer from his desk. He brought out €100,000 in cash and a check for €200,000, placing them on the desk with his handgun on top.

"I know where you all live and everything about you guys. If you fuck up, I'll come chasing after you and surely hunt you down. I do not have intentions of going to Liberia. I'm an ex-soldier. It won't be a good idea, but I have sent my boys and I have detailed reports of all the information I need," the old man boasted. He picked up the gun and pointed to Vitali.

"If anything goes wrong, next time this gun will be loaded and the little joke will be real." He dropped the gun, stood up and turned around to look through the window. "You may leave now."

The cab was at the gate in three minutes; dressed in a thick coat and a cap, Stanley looked like a real cab driver. As Vitali boarded the cab, holding the excitement with all his might, the old man peeked through the curtains, missing him already.

"Idiot, how far?" Stanley asked the white boy.

"I dey," he replied.

They drove some 30 minutes maintaining composure, hoping they were not followed. They stopped at a train station three towns away, abandoned the car and walked briskly to the waiting train. Luckily, they boarded as it was about to leave.

As they settled in, "How did it go?" asked Stanley.

"Wow!" he screamed – couldn't hold it anymore. Heads turned to look at them. "300K!" he whispered to his bud. "I forecast five million, man."

"Good, good, good job my boy. I knew you'd nail it." He adjusted himself and sat straight. "Let's maintain 'til we drop."

They remained calm, not talking much until they alighted in Viale Romagna. They exchanged bags, hailed different cabs and headed for an agreed-upon coffee shop. Stanley had everything planned. Vitali's cab headed straight for the shop while Stanley took a detour. He bought a small Alfa Romeo off a second-hand dealer and headed for the alley behind the coffee shop. Vitali left through the back door and got into the car. They drove the long journey to Venice talking about the job and all. Then, they called Don to inform him of their success.

**

"Asalam Aleikum."

"Hello, can I speak with Banji please?"

"OK, sir." Mahmud gave the phone to Banji. "It's Bros."

"Bros, how far? Are we on point? We established all protocols but didn't receive any visit."

"Pack your bags and come home. The job was smooth. You may ask the aboki *(friend)* to come have fun in Lagos."

"Sure, boss… but really, it happened just like that?" he asked.

"Pack your bags and come home."

"OK, boss!" he ended the call.

"We hit it, man, we've hammered!"

"Really?" Mahmud asked, sounding confused. "What do you mean?"

"The job went well."

"Really? Without all the protocols we prepared?"

"Dude, am I speaking German?"

"Yaay, alhamdulilah. 'Correct!' as you always say," They hugged and shook hands.

"Gimme a hand hug, man."

"What does that mean?"

Banji taught him, and they did it and played around the house in excitement.

***

Back in Naija, Brenda perfected all transactions, and deducted 12 percent of the lump sum. The remainder she split into two equal parts and transferred to the individual accounts of the two different parties.

Bros was big in the game, and his weight could not be compromised, otherwise Don would not share equal splits. From his share, Don squared Vitali 30 percent, 10 percent to Stanley, 10 percent to the boys and kept 50 percent. The journey just began. He informed his comrades, "This race is for 5 million."

"AWOO!" they all responded to his oration.

In Bros's camp, he squared the proprietor of the job – some young dude – 50 percent, gave Banji €5,000, Ace €2,000, and the Arab €2,000. He pocketed the remaining.

CHAPTER 7

Three months had passed, and the general was yet to stop paying. Money had been shared at the same ratio, and when other parties had to join in, adjustments were made, but the game had been played fairly. Integrity was a yardstick in this game; messing up could warrant brutal actions. In between, Don had visited his family once and spent two weeks with them. He had taken them on holiday to Miami and Disney World. It felt good being with family and away from the hustle, although he missed the game and thus ran things from wherever he was. He bought his wife a new set of jewelry, changed her car and saw to general needs. He was in a haste to return but kept his word and stayed the whole time.

Bros went back to the U.K. after the first split and continued to control his end from there; there had been no glitch, as his end was always tight. Banji continued in status quo. Ace had moved on with Ella; she had an enormous influence on him, positioning his thinking on positive things. He was freshly out of school and in pursuit of a career; Ella's uncle lured him into joining the NFCC. Initially he didn't buy the idea but then thought it wasn't going to take much off him if he spent a year or two on the force. An experience there would widen his scope and also protect him in anything he did. He would protect his friends, too, he had thought. He had taught Ella how to drive and given her his old car when she was good enough.

***

"I'd prefer snails; the vegetable soup garnished with plenty of shrimp. On the side, scramble some smoked fish in the porridge and don't forget to buy some *fufu* on your way. I'm as hungry as a starved lion!"

"OK, boss, gotcha!" she exclaimed. She hurriedly prepared the meals and stopped a cab to Lekki. She had been dating the whack rapper who hardly got any CDs sold. He paid loads to make himself some of the best videos on TV and to buy attention from the media. He rapped everything money but failed to earn a following; he wasn't well-informed on the Nigerian life on the streets. Besides, he had no business being a rapper.

A failed drug dealer in Spain, in and out of jail twice, he outsmarted his Jamaican boss, made away with plenty of euros and escaped to Nigeria. Fearing he could lose all the hard currency he flew in with, he bought a two-bedroom apartment, bought two mean machines and hurriedly integrated himself in the entertainment industry for cover-up. His cousin had advised him that it was better to be perceived as a scammer than a drug dealer in Lagos. He also suggested that feigning being an artist would be bought by the world. He further deceived him into believing he could rap. The sharp guy earned himself a cool 1999 Toyota Camry for his advisory services and loyalty. He learned some terms and registers and also acquainted quickly with leading boys around the hood.

Popularly known as Jasper, five-foot-nine and broad-chested with a six-pack from a lifelong obsession with the gym, he hurriedly grew a ponytail to give himself the prompt look of an *artiste*. He always dressed like there was a party. Seeing this cutie in a sickening argument with some guy while exiting a bar, he had stepped in and offered a fight. The bully easily let go. He wasn't ready to fight over some whore who pilfered his fabricated Hublot a couple of months earlier. Jasper offered her a ride, and she obliged. The one night they intended on spending together had turned into a sizzling love affair. Soon enough, they were virtually living together. The little scene with Don had killed her dreams with the man who meant the world to her. After frantic efforts at restoring normalcy, it wouldn't happen. She lost him.

I'm not going to lose this one, she told herself… *I will fight with everything in me to keep him.*

CHAPTER 8

Months had passed, and things had been really bad for Jasper. All the euros had been blown, with nothing coming in from music and scam. He had to sell one of his cars to survive and could barely maintain the other. His relationship with Queen had also been threatened severely. He wanted her to leave him, having concluded in his mind that he wouldn't be able to afford her high maintenance like he used to, but the smart Queen, realizing what was bothering him, had played her way with him smoothly. She had stopped demanding from him but would rather get from other men to give to him, claiming she had been getting funds from her folks or rich relatives.

He hadn't been convinced but he was left with no choice but to play along. They usually had heated arguments and would get into physical confrontations. They parted ways and got back together in the space of a few days. Things got really messy, but they patched it somehow.

"I think I need to start scamming, too," she announced to Jasper shortly after sex some evening.

He laughed. "What do you know about scam? I'm sure that you won't make a dollar in a whole year."

"Try me," she dared.

"Forget it, don't waste your time."

"I learned from the best. Loan me a laptop and a modem and watch what I can do in one month,"

she said to him confidently.

"Hmm," he stared at her cunningly, holding his jaw in his left hand, "You have a point there; I've heard of Ace, dude is good… You can have the other laptop, but I don't have money to buy you a modem. You'll have to get that yourself, but meanwhile, you can start with mine anytime I'm not using it."

"Thanks, baby," she kissed him and went down on him, but he turned her down, stepped out of bed and soaked himself in the bath.

Queen braced herself and danced to the soft music playing from the stereo. She tried some ballet any time she was excited about something.

***

"Dude!"

"Hey."

"Wassup baby, what you been up to?" Queen asked.

"Nothing much, making money all the way... That's all I ever do."

"Cool, Ace..."

"Yes?"

"I need a big favor from you..."

"I'm listening."

"I want to start yahoo..."

Ace burst into an intimidating laugh. And she cut in— "Erm, what's funny?"

"You amaze me, Queen… always."

"Duh! Ace, I'm not playing around, I need to make my own money, I need to hustle."

"We can't be together again babe, your decoy won't work; we've gone through all this. You need to move on."

"Fuck you!" She hung up and she wept.

Some forty minutes later, she decided to send an SMS to Ace.

"Dude, I'm sorry to bother you. I really need to do yahoo. I honestly don't want to depend on guys for money. I know you found love and I won't disturb you. All I need is for you to guide me through dating sites and a few things; I'll take it from there."

Ace calls back, "You're kidding, right?"

"I'm serious about this, trust me."

"What story do you want to feed your clients? You barely know anything in this game."

"I learned from the best. I learned from you."

"Right... I'll register profiles at different dating sites for you, get you pictures and send a comprehensive email containing virtually everything you need to know. You're on your own henceforth."

"Sure, boss!" she replied, really excited. She got to her feet and did some ballet. Four days later, she received a call from Ace.

"Check your email."

"Already? Great!"

She received an email alert on her phone as she hung up. She opened it to find a properly written and structured procedure. Included in the email were the following:

A dating site with username and password…

Yahoo Mail ID with username and password…

Gmail with username and password…

VPN with username and password…

United States social security number…

A zipped file containing 23 pictures of a Caucasian professional model…

A scanned copy of a California driver's license…

"Jasper!" she called and walked out of the kitchen to meet him playing a video game in the living room. "Ace sent in details. I'm starting work right away."

"Good for you," he said, barely acknowledging her.

She walked back to the kitchen mushy; she hastened up her cooking and sat at the dining table in the living room.

"The food is ready, you can help yourself."

Jasper pretended not to hear her and continued with his game.

"If you're hungry, you'll walk to the kitchen to serve yourself… fool!"

From where he was sitting, he threw the PS3 pad at her but missed. Getting up, he fiercely paced toward her. She got to her feet, ready for a fight. Jasper landed a big slap on her face that sent her sprawling on the floor, kicked her in the abdomen and bawled at her.

"If you try me further, I'll kill you...bitch!"

She remained on the floor sobbing. Jasper fetched some food and a beer, and then moved into the bedroom. Minutes later, he came out dressed up, picked up his car keys and walked out of the apartment. After he left, she took a quick shower and packed her things into a box. She picked up a laptop, the working modem and other things she would need. She briskly wheeled the box out of the building into the street and stopped a cab.

At home, she was warmly welcomed, but her mom soon saw the red on her face.

"What happened to you, Queen?" her mother asked. "Who did this to you?"

"It's Jasper," she answered and burst into tears.

Her mom held her in a warm embrace and wiped her tears with her wrapper. "It's OK, my baby, stop crying. You're home with Mommy, and no one can touch you here. Let me get you something to eat."

"I'm OK, Ma. I'm fine. I need to get some rest."

She woke up at 9.15 the next morning; her younger ones were off to school and dad, off to work. She was well-refreshed and stretched as she yawned.

"Good morning, Mommy."

"Good morning, how are you?"

"I'm fine, I feel very relaxed. I'll be home for some time – I have a lot to do and I need some time to myself."

Surprised, her mom asked her, "Is everything OK?"

"Of course, there's no problem, Ma. I just need time to myself and get my school work done. I won't be going out much and I don't want to be disturbed by the neighbours."

"OK, there's food in the pot. I have to go to my kiosk; I'm already late."

"Don't worry about me, I'll sort myself. Meanwhile, how is electricity in the neighbourhood?"

"We've not had electricity in three weeks, my daughter. Your father defaulted in paying the bills.

We've been cut off by the landlord."

"How much is the bill?"

"N2,500, I think. I was hoping to pay it if your father doesn't at the end of the week."

"Don't worry, I'll sort that out. Asides from that, is electricity regular?"

"It's regular at night only; we barely have electricity in the day."

"OK. What about the generator?"

"Your useless father sold it when he couldn't maintain it."

"It's OK, Mom, I'll buy a new one. I need to have constant electricity. You can go to the market now, I'll be fine."

They talked for some three minutes, and her mother left. She spent another three hours tidying up the two-room shack. Into three big sacks, she packed a whole lot of junk and threw them out. She arranged every other thing neatly, leaving the apartment looking lighter with the space that it lacked. She walked to the general bathroom to bathe. She dressed up, left the house and returned with a replica of the previous generator her dad had sold, the smallest and cheapest available. Queen got an electrical guy to check the wiring and also paid the owed electricity bill. Satisfied that everything was OK and the generator was running fine, she picked up her laptop and set it on the center table.

Her hustle began.

www.lovematchmaker.com. The ad boasted, "If we don't find you that special someone in a fortnight, you'll get your money back."

Cool, I love this site already, she thought to herself. *Moneykid always talks about it.* She took her time to peruse the site, studying and analyzing the number of men living in California. The ones who indicated their income she highlighted as priority by writing their usernames in a separate folder on her desktop. She took her time to study each profile and made brief details on each of them.

Ace had built her a good profile. Her profile name was Butterflies Inside.

Headline: Love is all that matters.

Brief Story: I believe I'm cute, dutiful and cuddly. I love sand and sun and horse riding too. I've been hurt before, no time for players and low lives. I'm on this site for serious minded men only, scammers beware… I can be a bitch too. I can't wait for my Knight in shining armor, only him I want to share my life with. Whoop whoop, I really can't wait to meet you!!! xoxo.

State: California
City: Palmdale
Occupation: Nurse
Income: $25, 000 - $50,000
Relationship status: Single
Children: None
Age: 24
Accommodation: Shared apartment
Education: College
Race: Caucasian
Religion: Not important
Sexuality: Straight
Diet: Normal
Willing to relocate: Anywhere in the world

She extended her search to other states, Canada, the United Kingdom, Australia and Cyprus. By the time she was done, all her family was already asleep. She had barely spoken to anyone. She had only welcomed them and asked how the day went. If they tried to speak further, she would tell them she was busy. The routine was on for the next few days, and her family giving her the space she needed. She switched off her phone also, chatting only with Ace and asking him questions whenever he came online. He often ignored her, though, usually reminding her she was on her own.

Her profile picture and story attracted some suitors, spammers mostly. She clicked the ignore button on the spammers and responded to those she perceived were legitimate. She sent winks to her prospects and received emails in return.

Her first reply was a default response.

Thanks for your email, really glad you did.

I'd like us to continue our conversation through email or yahoo messenger.

My email is butterflyjennylove@yahoo.com, please respond asap. Can't wait to know you better.

The emails kept coming, and she got busy responding with the pre-written letters she got from Ace. She only had to edit certain details and names. She seemed pretty excited now that things were going smoothly. She relaxed a bit and chatted a little more with her family when they returned home. She also extended her courtesy to the neighbors, although not spending too much time with them.

Day six, she woke up at 7.35 a.m., really excited, believing it was a good day to ask one of her suitors for money. She prayed fervently on the severely patched three-seater sofa that served as her bed. Her younger ones lay on a mat snoring. It was a Saturday, and no one was in a hurry to go out. She stared at her laptop, tempted to turn it on but said to herself, *Dick won't be online until 2 p.m. Nigerian time / 8 a.m. in California.*

She headed to the bedroom, walking over her brothers. Her mom was awake already and tidying up.

"Good morning, Mama."

"How are you, Queen? What will you have for breakfast?"

"Don't worry, Mama. I'll do the cooking today. What would you like to have?"

"Beancake and pap will be fine."

"OK, Mama."

She opened the cupboard where foodstuff was stored, picked two empty bowls and packed enough beans into one. She walked back to her sofa, settled down and began to pick the chaff and stones from the beans. Her brothers woke up while she was at it and they offered to help but she declined, asking them to have a field day. Her father came to the living room and sat beside her. He had really missed her, and they indulged in long conversations and gossip. He joined in the picking of the beans on his insistence.

The mood was light that day; the younger men watched TV, and their mother got engrossed in her chores. Queen washed the beans, soaked them in water for a while and peeled off the skins. This she did several times till she was satisfied. She poured the clean skinned beans into a five-liter paint bucket that had been converted to kitchen use and left the home for the neighbourhood grinding mill. It was only five blocks from her home. She was dressed in a bumper short and a half T-shirt with no bra. She smiled and greeted everyone in return.

The neighbourhood mill was a little shop at the entrance of a very populated three-story building with a small fabricated grinder powered by a petrol motor. She met a queue of six girls. The girls were happy to see her. They called her by her real name and they talked extensively. They admired her beauty, as they always did, some even called her *Oyinbo* (Caucasian). They asked her of the beauty products she was using and stuff about boys, school and all. They were really happy that Queen gave them that much audience.

She ground her beans and left. Some of the girls walked her to her house as the talk intensified. At her apartment door, she told them she had to get busy and that she would see them later in the day. Queen prepared breakfast, and everybody ate. Because she was not so comfortable using the laptop on the center table, she decided to buy a plastic table and chair. She positioned the chair and table by the living room window, which was directly opposite the door. That way, she sat backing the window and faced the door. The three-seater sofa was to her right, and to her left was an old cabinet that housed their old TV, radio and other petty stuffs. At the end of the cabinet was the bedroom door. Between the bedroom door and the living room door was a dilapidated couch.

She was not happy with the living condition of her family, but there was nothing she could do to change that right now. Sitting by her plastic makeshift desk gave her a clearer view of her home.

We are really poor, she reminded herself and vowed to change everything. At 1.27 p.m. she was ready; she had bathed and was wearing fresh shorts and a T-shirt. Her parents were out, and her brothers were also out to play. She put on her laptop and smiled, loving the peace and quiet. She logged onto her Yahoo Messenger profile but found no offline messages. She was online until 5.15 a.m., when her online prospects went to bed. The messenger indicated she had 14 emails. She clicked on the icon, and her Yahoo Mail was launched on her Mozilla. She read through the email subjects, and her jaw dropped as she saw one of the emails from www.lovematchmaker.com.

In bold characters, the subject read: YOUR ACCOUNT IS DECLINED.

"Shit!!!" she screamed, "What did I fucking do wrong?" She clicked on the email, clicked a new tab and opened the dating site. As she was about to investigate what happened, someone knocked on the door. Still baffled with the unfortunate development, she yelled with the highest pitch of her voice, "Who the fuck is that?"

Realizing she was over-reacting, she calmed herself, walked to the door and asked in a better tone, "Who's that?"

"It's me," the subtle masculine voice declared.

Not knowing who the person was, she opened anyway. It happened to be one of the many guys from the neighbourhood who were crushing on her. The guy was dressed in his best T-shirt and jeans, wearing cheap perfume and a lame swag.

"What do you want?" she asked calmly.

"I came to see you."

"For what?" She was still struggling to hold her calm.

"It's been a long time, babe, I miss you. Won't you ask me to come in? Let's relate."

Now furious, Queen looked at him from his head to his feet and warned him never to come by her door or talk to her if he should see her on the streets. She banged the door shut on him and walked back to her desk. She keyed in her username and password on the dating site, an unfriendly page came up with an even more unfriendly statement: Your account has been declined due to fraudulent activities. She opened the emails from her prospects; some called her bitch and other swear names. Some wrote lengthy emails advising her to get a life. Two emails were encouraging, though; apparently they were yet to know she had been banned from the site. She mustered some conviction and replied to them with the hope that things wouldn't go wrong. After responding to the emails, she returned to Yahoo Messenger and dropped offline messages to Dick, Garry and Lionel. These guys were the ones with most potential.

To Dick she wrote:

Good morning hun, you were in my dreams all night...gosh, what have you done to me, I can't stop thinking about you

Wish I am in your arms right now, I want to kiss you and make good and passionate love to you

I also made breakfast...omelets fried in fat-free butter, toast and some Indian tea with cream. You should be here with me baby, I will overfeed you

I will have a dozen babies for you and we will live happily ever after

Buzz me when you're online, I'm not far from my p.c.

She copied Garry and Lionel the exact words she sent to Dick and checked Ace's messenger. His pseudonym showed offline. Frustrated, she turned her phone on and was met with a backlog of text messages, BBM messages, email alerts, Facebook alerts, tweets and other alerts. She dialed Ace's number, which went busy after it rang for a second. She tried repeatedly and the same happened.

He's with his girlfriend, she thought and stopped calling. Jasper's number appeared as an incoming call; she let it ring. "I'm done with this idiot, I'll never go back to him," she said aloud. At the second ring, she ended his call. He doesn't stop calling and she continued to end it. Tired of his unrelenting calls, she switched off her phone and dropped it on her desk. She walked out of the apartment to the hallway and knocked on the last door on her wing. An aging woman opened the door, and Queen bought a bottle of Coke. By the time she was back at her desk, she had messages from Dick. She was happy to see that Dick was yet to find out she had been kicked off the dating site, and she read:

Dick: *Hey love…*
Daddy's here
Don't keep an old man waiting for love
Talk to me honey
Butterflies:
Hello baby
I'm here…good morning
Dick:
Good morning love, sleep well?
Butterflies:
Yes I did *smile*
Dick:
Awesome!!!

I want breakfast right now, and the kisses and the love making

I need everything like yesterday

The 64-year-old retired truck driver said in anxiety, surprised to receive seductive notes already from this young girl of his dreams.

Butterflies:

Say the magic word

Dick:

Open sesame?

Butterflies:

I'm all urs

I can take a week off from work but I have to give a minimum of two weeks' notice

Dick:

*Do that right away! *wink**

Butterflies:

Will do that on Monday

Dick:

*Great!! counting down!!! *biggrin**

Can't wait to see you in person

*I will take you into the mountains in my Monster F-650, there are great views up there *wink**

We'll have a picnic and drink beer

Afterward, I'll take you to the lake in my county and I will catch for you the biggest fish in the pond!

I will treat you like a goddess and make you happy in every way I can

Butterflies:

*Cool! I can't wait!!! *smile**

One second hun, I got a call
Dick:
Ok darling, not going anywhere.

Queen stared at her laptop for a few seconds, her mind racing. She contemplated making a move on the old man before he knew something was wrong. She switched her phone on and called Ace endlessly, but he didn't succumb. Three minutes gone, she got to her feet and paced around the living room.

Dick:
I'll make coffee

After eight minutes since her last note to Dick she finally braced herself and sat back at her desk.

Butterflies:
Hey baby, I'm back!
Dick:
Honey I'm here, coffee tastes good
What took you so long?
Butterflies:
There's an emergency
Dick:
Tell me
Butterflies:
I won't bother you with my problems honey
Dick:
I insist!
Butterflies:
You win
My 16-year-old cousin rode his bike into an old lady's delivery

It is expensive glassware and she threatens to press charges of burglary if she's not refunded by noon

The invoice indicates a total of $3,245. My aunt has been able raise $2,100 and all I have right now is $700 *sad*

Don't know what to do arrgggg!!

There's a long pause from Dick.

Are you there honey, told you I didn't want to bother you with my problems.

Dick eventually responds:

I'll send $500

But you will have to buy your flight ticket to Ohio when you get that week off *wink*

Queen froze; she barely believed what was happening. She looked to the ceiling and thanked God briefly. A teardrop rolled down her cheek.

Butterflies:

God bless your kind soul *kiss* *kiss* *kiss*"

Dick:

Send me details. *biggrin*

Butterflies:

Ok boss!

5 minutes

Queen hurriedly sent an SMS to Ace "Mugu *(client)* wants to pay, send details or go to Yahoo." She also copied her conversation with Dick to Ace's Yahoo Messenger. Ace called back immediately and asked, "How much?"

Queen responded excitedly, "500."

"Cool! You're doing pretty well. Didn't expect you'll turn out this smart... I think you're merely lucky."

"Your problem, Ace. Send me details right now."

"Ok, Yahoo Queen." He got on his laptop and logged on his messenger. He read the conversation between Queen and Dick and smiled. "She's smart after all." He opened a folder on his desktop and copied something.

Queen received his message.

AceOfThePack:

Barbra Windeck

205, Norton Avenue

San Francisco

CA 55231

Butterflies:

Awesome!

Thanks a lot darling...I miss you

Ace didn't reply. She copied Dick.

Butterflies:

Barbra Windeck

205, Norton Avenue,

San Francisco

CA 55231

Dick:

Got it

What do I do with this?

Butterflies:

Send Western Union

Dick:

How? Never done this before

Does she not have a bank account I can pay into?
Queen fumes.
Butterflies:
It's an instant way of wiring money
She'll receive it immediately you send it
Gimme your zip code and I'll look for the nearest
one to you
Dick:
Oh! Forgive me honey
Now I know what you're talking about...there's one
at the retail shop down the road.
Butterflies:
Awesome! *smile* *hug*
Send me the details when you're done or scan the
receipt to me
I have to run now...will send my quota to her right
away!
Dick:
Call her before you leave and ask her to hang in
there, tell her Dick is to the rescue *cowboyhat*
Butterflies:
Ok hun

Queen jumped off her seat and screamed for joy.
She did some ballet.

Dick got off his desk also; he was dressed in white
briefs and white vest. He selected a pair of blue jeans
from a rack and wore them. He opened his closet
and picked the left foot of a rancher's boot, brought
out a thick wool sock, and squeezed a fat roll of $50
bills. He removed the rubber band, straightened the
money, and walked back to his desk. He spat a little on

his right thumb and forefinger and placed each note on his desk in a parallel pattern as he counted slowly: 1,2,3,4,5,6,7,8,9,10.

Dick tied the remaining money back in a roll with the rubber band and placed it on the desk. He gathered the 10 bills into a stack and recounted. Convinced it was all $500, he put the roll back in its initial place, picked up a pen and wrote the recipient's details boldly on a jotter. This sheet, he tore off, neatly placed the bills in it, folded in two and placed them in his jeans pocket.

Fully dressed in his regular boots, denim jacket and hat, he returned to his PC and wrote:

Dick:

*Got the cash, I'm on my way to Western Union, love you hunny. *kiss* *kiss**

He walked out of his condo into the yard, climbed into his truck and drove into town.

Queen didn't touch her laptop; Ace always talked about leaving his desktop in idle mode whenever he told a *mugu* he was away from his computer. She picked up her phone and sent Ace an SMS: "He's gone to make the payment... yippee!"

It was the longest hour in Queen's life. While she waited, she drank three bottles of Coke, prayed, did ballet, watched TV, listened to radio, tweeted, Facebooked and more. She counted every minute as it passed. When it was exactly 40 minutes since her last message to Dick, she convinced herself she had burned enough time to have made her own end of the payment. She notified Dick and buzzed him a couple of times. Eventually, she asked Dick to buzz her when he got back and she returned to status quo.

1 hour and 26 minutes later…

Dick:

Are you there?

Queen restrained herself for 80 seconds.

Butterflies:

Hey honey, I'm here

How did it go?

Dick:

Tell me who you truly are.

Butterflies:

Lol…what do you mean?

Dick:

Be honest with me…I still love you

Butterflies:

Of course you know who I am

Dick:

Why is your profile declined from the dating site?

I looked you up and I'm told you're a fraud.

Are you a con artist? Tell me the truth and I will forgive you.

Queen exclaims, "Chineke (God)! Alarm don blow (He's caught me)!"

Butterflies:

What do you mean by that…have you been snooping on me?

Now I know you don't trust me!

Remember I never wanted to tell you about this issue…I'd have found a way around it myself.

Queen placed a call to Ace. "The old man has found out it's a scam!"

"How do you mean?" Ace asked.

"My account has been declined from the site."

"Fuck! How did that happen?"

"I don't know."

"I've been on that site for three years, and nothing has gone wrong. What about the money?"

"I don't think he made the payment."

"Save your chat history. I'll login from my laptop," Ace said.

"How do I do that?" Queen asked.

"Fool! Do you ever know anything? All you have in your head is prick and money!" He instructed her on how to go about it. Ace logged in as Butterflies from his messenger.

Butterflies:

Sorry hun, Internet issues

Dick:

I want to see you on cam

Butterflies:

We've been over all that

Dick:

I won't send the money

Butterflies:

Don't worry about it, I'll find a way

Dick:

Let me know when you have the holiday, I'll send you a ticket

Butterflies:

I'll sure do that, can't wait to meet you eventually

Dick:

Bye for now

Butterflies:

Bye sugar

Ace read through the history and called Queen. "What did you do wrong?"

Queen responded, "I don't know, I followed all your instructions."

"OK, I usually don't do small amounts but I wanted you to have that money. That old man has the potential of paying you more than $20,000, but you flopped." He cursed under his breath.

"Wait a minute; did you use the VPN I gave you?"

"What's VPN?" she asked.

"Dammit! Don't ever call me again!" And he hung up.

Queen cried for a while, braced up and went out. She boarded a commercial motorbike to a bar not so far from home but far enough not to be recognized. She smoked half a pack of cigarettes and drank four bottles of Smirnoff Ice. She went back home and didn't talk to anyone. She just lay on her sofa and plugged her phone's hands-free into her ears and slept off.

The next day, Sunday, she barely spoke to anyone, ate little and slept most of the day. Nobody dared ask what was wrong with her. She woke up to excruciating noise; the couple next door picked their fights mostly on Monday mornings when the husband couldn't provide transportation and feeding for children to go to school. It was 7.25 a.m. Her brothers were just leaving for school.

"You guys won't holla at your sis before leaving for school?"

"Not so, we don't want to disturb your sleep."

"It's OK," she responded, "Get my bag." She gave them N500 each; they were really excited and bounced happily to school. Her mother came out of the bedroom, and they spoke for a while. Her dad also emerged and headed to work, leaving the two women. Queen relieved her mom of her chores, and she left for her kiosk. After tidying the house, Queen had her bath and made some thick hot cocoa. She sat by her desk and put on her laptop. Queen was bewildered as she found out her screen was half covered in ink.

"God, why are you doing this to me? Do I deserve this much pain," she cried. "I am nice to everyone but I get ill-treated in return. I'll skin those boys when they return from their silly school!"

For a while, she remained, thinking of what to do. She picked up her phone and sieved through the messages she had ignored. Jasper had been begging, girlfriends had been missing her, random guys hitting on her but Don had sent a short note: "Call me." He had called twice.

She pondered on what to do. Her cash had virtually run out and she was stuck with no tools for her new venture. She was tempted to call Don, knowing she'd earn a chunk of money if she obliged his invitation to the mansion, but the guilt of losing Ace to her gullibility the last time sickened her. She decided to call Ace.

"Wassup," the big-talker voice said slowly on the other side.

She melted and hesitated for two seconds. "Hey babe, can I talk to you for a minute?"

"Go ahead, Queen, I'm listening." She was sure he was high. It was how he sounded whenever he had smoked marijuana.

"I'm sorry I messed up on the job."

"It's OK, Queen, you actually tried. You pulled that ish in less than two weeks init?"

"Five days, actually."

"That's remarkable! I don't do small monies like that, but it's a good start for a rookie."

She blushed.

"I set up a new profile for you last night. This time don't blow it... use the VPN."

"I won't mess up this time, honey. I miss you, Ace."

"Don't start," he said firmly. It was almost an order.

"My laptop is broken, though; it fell down the stairs, I ..."

"I'll credit your account with 150k. Buy yourself a new laptop."

"Oh ma God, oh ma God, you're kidding right?"

"Don't forget to use your VPN. If you got issues, holla." He dropped the call.

Queen was dumbfounded and lost in space as she gazed at the door before her. Her phone rang.

"I can't find your account details on my phone. Send it now." He hung up.

She sent it. Six minutes later, she received an alert and began to sob.

CHAPTER 9

"By the powers conferred on me by the Federal Government of Nigeria, I congratulate all of you for the courage and perseverance you have shown in the past months. You have convinced us through physical, academic and intellectual tests that you are capable and worthy of the position of junior cadets. You are all welcome to the Nigerian Financial Crimes Commission. I believe you will all do your country proud."

Gun salutes filled the air with the NFCC anthem playing in the background by the police band. A crowd was cheering. The new graduates congratulated one another as they broke off the lines they had maintained the past three hours in the blazing hot afternoon sun.

Ace fetched his phone from his pocket and rang Ella. "Where you at, sweets?"

"Under the mango trees, it's a yellow tent... you won't miss it."

"Great!" he responded in high spirits as he moved to locate her. They hugged tightly and kissed for a minute.

"I miss you, sweetheart," Ace said.

"I miss you more," Ella replied.

Ace turned to his buddy and hugged him; he tilted him off the ground and put him down. They did the hand hug.

"Short man, I'm really glad you came."

"It's nothing, brother, I wouldn't miss this event for anything, man." Banji answered.

Ace now met with his family; they were all happy for him and greeted him warmly.

***

Ace had spent the past months training to become an agent. It had been rough in the beginning, especially with the physical training. He became the favorite of a couple of senior agents when he displayed unusual intelligence on Internet scams. He confided in Bala, who showed the most interest in him about his past involvement in the scam underworld. Bala made sure he skipped most physical activities by assigning him to cadet official duties. It wasn't long before he was introduced to the training commandant.

At first, he wasn't particularly comfortable with the preferential treatment he was getting; he gladly played along with the indulgence. What intrigued him most was that he was never queried for information about his shady past but rather won himself a gold ticket with the chiefs. He smartly requested to be posted to Lagos, even though he was promised a profitable position in Abuja. Ace had his own plans.

***

After taking pictures at the grounds, they had lunch at the Sheraton Hotel, Abuja. Ace's dad drove them to the airport and bid them farewell. Ace hugged his mom and kissed her on the cheek; he hugged his brother and shook his hand.

"I'll be home on Sunday, Mom… I need to hang with my boys."

"Enjoy your weekend, TGIF," his mom replied with a broad smile. The two parties greeted and dispersed in two separate cars.

***

Ace marveled as Banji opened the remote controlled gate.

"No, no, no, no… this is not yours man, it must be Bros's. This can't be true, mate."

"It's what it is, man. Welcome to the Manor of Banji the Great!"

"This is awesome, bro!" Ace exclaimed as he grabbed Banji's head with two hands and shook it. Banji pulled up by the front door of the four-bedroom detached house. Although there was ongoing renovation to the exterior of the building, it was evident that it was a beautiful structure judging by its twin. Bros had recently evicted the previous tenant, who owed 17 months' rent. Because of Banji's unending sojourn in hotel rooms, he offered to sell him the house if he had a down payment of 10 million naira, the remaining 25 million naira to be paid over two years. Wasteful Banji had just a little over four million naira in his bank account; he was able to make his dad support him with 6 million naira. It was a modest offer for the lucky dude, as the market value of the house was 120 million naira.

He ushered Ace and Ella into the living room and bolted the big iron and glass door. He walked them through the unfurnished parlor; they climbed the stairs, and he showed them to their room.

"I bought the mattress and installed the air conditioning for you two days ago – please bear with me; it's not easy to set up a home," he said.

"Man…you're doing pretty well, and I'm impressed. I'll sleep on the floor as long as it's your home, bro."

"That's my room," he pointed to his door. "Need to have a quick shower."

He had barely left the room when the visitors shut the door behind them and began to kiss. They hadn't had sex with each other in months and could barely wait. It was a quick one, but very relished. They got in the shower, but water wouldn't flow. Ace stepped out of the room nude and opened Banji's door.

"Guy, there's no water in the shower… Guy, are you there?" He checked in the bathroom and exited the room. At the door, he met the short man. "Dude… you bad! I see you guys couldn't hold it for long. I had to start the generator to pump water – must have left a tap running when I left home in the morning."

"OK." Ace walked back to his girlfriend, and they did it again. Exhausted and hungry, they showered again and wore fresh clothes. Ella left the room in boxers and a white vest she got from Ace's bag and went in search of the kitchen. Ace followed in blue joggers and a black T-shirt. They found the supposed kitchen downstairs empty but for the inbuilt furniture. Ace chuckled.

"This nigga will never be serious."

They climbed the stairs and knocked on Banji's door.

"Come in."

They met him smoking a cigarette and peeking into a small fridge.

"Dude, you have to build yourself a kitchen and find a girl that will cook you good meals. You can't continue like this."

"I know. She has complained about it also," he responded.

"Are you serious?" Ella asked, her eyes full of sarcasm. "Don't tell me you now have a girlfriend."

"Of course I do, she'll be coming around later in the day."

"Wow, I find it hard to believe, but it's a good thing..."

Ace cut in, "He's probably broke." The trio burst into laughter.

"I can never go broke, mate, you know I'm a moneymaker. The country will go broke before guys like me can smell such," Banji said, boasting.

He actually *was* broke. They nibbled on junk from his fridge and changed clothing. Ace wanted to have *amala*; he hadn't had any since he left for camp. After dinner they picked up Kemmie, Banji's new girlfriend, and went to a nice bar, where they talked as family. Ella and Kemmie got along quite well and agreed to be best friends for life. They ignored the guys and did some catching up on themselves.

The boys left them at the table and walked toward the bar.

***

"Now that you've become an agent, what are your plans like?"

"Man, I'm really not sure... I think I did it to satisfy Ella. I'm still in the game and I will be forever."

"That's good to know. I've been worried about you since you picked up this new episode. I thought I lost you for good."

"Of course not, Banj. We're brothers forever regardless of what vocation either of us may choose. Besides, we all need someone to be on the other side... you never know."

"Good thinking, you'll easily clean out our dirty cache or get us out of trouble. Boys are longing to see you, man – they want to throw a party for you," Banji said.

"That won't be a good idea, though; I got to keep it low. They've been calling, but not sure I want anyone to know I'm in town yet. Besides, I got a lot of work to do. I've been away from the game for too long. Got some jobs I left unattended. I've got two weeks break, enough time to make some cheez, nigga!"

"That's wassup, Ace… now I know we're still blood," Banji said, sighing.

"Blood forever, man, you're my brother from another mother," replied Ace.

They shook hands and hugged.

"What's new on the town, bro? I'm a little rusty from my sojourn. You need to fill me in on new stuff … and, yes, where the money for the house came from."

"About the house, Bros sold it to me half-price; got Pop to support me with it. What's left of it has two years grace of paying up."

"That's awesome, bro, that's really great. Bros is a really cool guy; I'll root for him anytime."

"He's too nice to me. Without him, I'd probably be eating crumbs… he opens big doors for me, man."

"I know," Ace agreed, "I'd have hooked you up with my game though, if you didn't know Bros."

"Man, you guys are geniuses. I don't think I can. Don't have the patience to sit for months chatting with whoever; I'll probably die from depression."

"Naaa, it's not what you think. If you started the hustle with dating scams, you'd probably find it hard to do other stuff. Take a random look at all the boys you know, you'll notice that it's tough for guys to blend into other scams asides what they are used to. Let's look at artisans… a trained mechanic will find it hard to blend in as a carpenter even if he has to learn from the scratch."

"True talk, Ace."

"You're lucky to have Bros. He does all the work and gives you leads. All you do is execute. What I'll advise is that you learn a little something of your own, or make more big contacts should anything go wrong."

"Nothing will go wrong, bro. Besides, I know a lot of contacts. Bros has hooked me up with a lot of his business associates. It can only get better," Banji declared. "That reminds me, Don asked about you a week ago. He wants you to call him when you're back from training."

"That tiny fool, I should break his nose if I see him."

"Take it easy, man. Don't blame the guy over Queen," Banji tapped Ace on the back and held him on the shoulder, "He wouldn't have done Queen if he knew she was with us. It was probably some random hook-up."

"True talk."

"But, dude, you still love Queen. It shows in your eyes."

"Hell no, I can't love a bitch. I'm happy about the other day… it was an eye-opener. I always thought I would end up marrying her. My mom loves her to death. She still asks about her."

"You know how girls are these days. It's probably age stuff and peer influence. It's their hustle, you know."

"Hustle, my ass… I gave her everything she needed man. She had no reason to do shits. Well she's started doing yahoo too, I taught her."

"Really? That's good to know. That should keep her occupied." Banji said, sounding really surprised.

"Hey boys," Ella cut in. "You guys have left your gentleman chips in the car, I presume. I can go get them for you."

Ace and Banji laughed.

"So sorry, sweets, forgive our manners… I miss this dude so much," declared Banji.

They got back to the table and left about an hour later.

CHAPTER 10

9.45 Monday morning, a knock came on the door.

"Who is it?" Queen asked.

"It's me," a female voice responded.

"Who are you?" Queen stressed.

"K.C."

Surprised, Queen hurriedly got up from her sofa and looked around the living room. Satisfied there was no litter, she picked up her pillow and bed sheet and threw them into the bedroom. She straightened up and opened the door. They screamed and hugged each other, checked themselves out and hugged again. Queen dragged her in, guided her to sit with a little push and stood in front of her gesticulating and admiring her clothes and hair.

"Babe, this is a big surprise. To what do I owe this surprise? You're looking really beautiful."

"I miss you Queen... a lot! I miss your presence in school, too."

"I miss you more, babes. I suddenly lost it for school, babes. I got busy hustling."

"I've asked you to come back to school several times; yahoo is for boys."

"K.C., I'm getting better every day. Trust me. I'm going to be rich!"

"I trust you will, hun, but don't play with school while you're at it. Yahoo should be a pastime. With school, you've got something to fall back to if other things fail. Your certificate will become your passport for life."

"I know, babes, but you know I'm not really cut out for school."

"Who says... you know I always got your back."

"Yea, babes, it's not as easy as you think."

"Have you considered your parents?"

Now uncomfortable, Queen said with a little edgy tone, "Leave them out of this, please... It's not like they pay my fees anyway."

"I'm sorry, Queen, let's flip this chapter."

They talked about other stuffs. Queen tried to show off what she had been doing on her laptop, but uninterested K.C. unwillingly made comments. Queen had been on her quest for months with no remuneration; she had labored endlessly and untiring. There were times she gave up but then found encouragement from within or the dream of a Mercedes CLK that never left her thoughts. She was really broke and barely left the apartment. Her ever-busy phone had been silent too. While making tea for K.C., her phone suddenly began to ring.

Startled, she hastily went for it. She looked at the caller ID and wore a displeasured look.

"Who is it?" K.C. asked.

"Don."

"Why that look?"

"You know why, babes."

"So? Are you still dating Ace?"

"Don killed my relationship with him."

"Look who's talking... big slut." K.C. said with sarcasm, "It's not like you didn't cheat on Ace with other men. You better take his call... You need all the money you can get right now... Your beauty is fading already."

"I want to make my own money."

"How much have you made so far? You got to survive, Queen; besides, I think he likes you a lot."

"He does..." She picked his call at the third ring, "Hey shorty!"

"You're avoiding me," Don said subtly.

"Not what you think, I've been busy with..."

"I'm in Lagos, meet me at the Royale for six."

"OK."

Don hung up.

"I have to see him at six," Queen told K.C.

"Good, now we have to put you back into shape."

"Don't have money to make my hair."

"I'll sort that out. Go and have your bath, then let's hit the town, baby!"

"Great!" She served K.C. some tea and left for the bedroom to pack a bag. From there, she went for a bath.

**

Don was welcomed by Efe at the MM2 Airport in Lagos with a big black umbrella. They walked briskly into the back door of the white S500 Benz. The driver hurried to his seat and drove off.

"The turbulence was heavy through the flight, man. I've never been that scared in my life."

"Don? Scared? How am I to believe that?"

"God is with me anyway, no shakes."

"Now, that's the Don talking!"

They waded through the wet Lagos traffic for some two hours. The driver halted at the entrance of the Platinum Bank and drove off to find a parking space after the two bosses alighted and walked into the building. They signed the visitor's log and rode the gold-plated elevator to the 13th floor where they met waiting Brenda. They discussed for a while and were later joined by a squat middle-aged man who came in with some documents they attended to. They rounded up in some 50 minutes and rode down the elevator excited.

It was a fine evening as the sun set behind beautiful architecture to the west of the magnificent Hotel Royale. The Toyota Corolla yellow cab awaited its turn at its gates. Four cars had passed, and the cab halted for routine screening. The driver received a ticket that permitted vehicles a maximum of one hour free parking and maneuvered through the four acres of neatly arranged parking lot.

Following the arrows hung four feet from the base of the trees that stood tall on both sides of the interlocked road, it pulled up at the hotel's massive entrance. The fabulous Queen stepped out, one black suede high heel at a time, revealing long, fair-skinned legs and then the enchanting frame of a very beautiful young woman. She was dressed in a very short black skirt and an off-white tube top loosely covered by a blue denim jacket. Slowly, she removed her Miu Miu sunglasses and tucked them safely in her cleavage as she approached the big rotating glass. As she stretched to push the door open, a tall, clean-looking elderly man – possibly in his sixties – paced up and swung the glass.

"Permit me," he said and ushered her in.

She smiled lightly and walked into the lobby. The man met her halfway to the reception, then bent over and whispered in her ear, "You're one hell of a beautiful being."

She went a little red on her cheeks and responded, "Thank you."

"Can I meet you?" he asked.

"Queen."

"You're a beautiful Queen," he told her and handed her a complimentary card. "Be free to call me during working hours."

"I will," she said with a broad smile, and the gentleman walked to the elevator.

She spoke to one of the receptionists, "Hello... room 305 please."

"Your name?"

"Queen."

"One second, please…" the receptionist said with a smile, admiration in her eyes. On the big screen at the reception, a story on E! drew Queen's attention, and she gazed with some attention.

"The guest in 305 is not picking my calls. You may want to call him on your phone or wait for five minutes for me to try again," the receptionist informed her.

"Don't worry, I'll wait," Queen said, really engrossed in the story. Six minutes later, she fetched her phone from her bag and called Don. "I'm here," she spoke into the mouthpiece.

The receptionist's phone rang immediately. She turned to Queen after answering the call. "Third floor, third room on the left."

"Thank you," Queen said and walked to the elevator.

As the elevator doors slid open on the third floor, she saw the same elderly man running through the hallway with his jaw in his hands. Bewildered, she paused for a second and then tried to utter a word. The man headed towards the elevator, but the doors shut before he reached them. He then turned to the stairs and dashed out of sight. Still stunned, Queen paused some 10 seconds before walking to 305.

She knocked on the door and cautiously walked in as a tall, slightly-built guy in his late twenties opened it. In the room, another guy was standing by the window. She noticed they were all looking very tense but she managed to conceal her fear. The little man walked towards her and spread his arms for an embrace, which she obliged, although a little reluctantly. He introduced her to the young guy, Charles, and Efe, who was a bit taller than Don, but rotund with a potbelly. She noticed Don kept massaging his knuckles.

"Can you please wait for me in 309, honey? I'll be with you in a minute," Don excused her, offering a card key from his breast pocket. He pecked Queen on the cheek and handed her the key. Twenty minutes later, he joined her. He tried to woo her and get her excited. Don began to profess love to her, telling her how he had missed her and all. He further offered to take her out, but she declined. She refused to give in to sex, either.

***

"We're at the hotel, boss," Banji said into his mobile phone while driving into the hotel.

"Wait for me at the restaurant, I'll be with you in 10 minutes," Don responded. He was dressed already. Queen, still lazing in bed, watched him leave the room. At the door, he turned swiftly, as if to catch her stare. He told her he would be right back and blew her a kiss.

It was 8.45 Tuesday morning. The restaurant was sparsely attended, with a few dotted people on some of the tables. He spotted Banji and Ace and joined them. They rose to their feet to greet him. All shook hands, and Don asked them to sit.

"Breakfast?" he asked.

"Sure," the two young guys responded.

"You guys are on time; you must have left home early," he said, smiling sheepishly, avoiding eye contact with Ace.

"We live 20 minutes away from here, boss. Bros sold me his house in Oniru," Banji said.

"Nice, your brother is really a nice guy. That's really good to know, Banji." He broadened his smile, stretched a hand and shook Banji's. "Congratulations, young man. I'm really happy for you."

Banji gesticulated in his chair, "Yes, boss," and threw a salute.

Immediately, Don relapsed into a sober state, managing to look at Ace before he said, "Before we go on, I'd like us to clarify something."

Ace and Banji responded simultaneously, "OK, boss."

"I'm sorry about your girlfriend, Queen. I sincerely would not have done stuff with her if I knew she was with you..." he said, making sure he was using the right words.

Ace cut in, "Forget about her, Don. Girls are the same – they are all bitches, especially Queen. I now have me a cute good girl and I'm happy."

"Great," Don said, hiding his emotions behind the pretext of sipping hot tea. "Now we have a truce, I believe."

"There's nothing to worry about. Let's talk business," Ace said, assuring him.

Banji concurred.

"Good, then." Don began, "A cousin of mine is held by your people. He's been locked up in Abuja for over three weeks.

"What did he do?" Ace asked.

"He ran a local scam on some businessman."

"Hmm... Is it connected to any form of murder?" Ace asked.

"Nooo, he's a good boy. He specializes in paperwork. You won't find him associated with violence," Don said, sounding convincing.

"How much is it?"

"Thirty million," Don answered.

"Is the money safe or has it been seized?"

"It's with me."

"My people will demand a 30 to 40 percent cut, boss. I have to know if you are OK with that."

"It's not a problem Ace. I know how it works."

"Cool, give me a second, boss," Ace said and brought out his phone.

He called Bala and filled him in.

"Can you make it to Abuja before 2 p.m.?" Bala asked. "I'll be traveling tomorrow morning."

Ace covered his phone mouthpiece and asked Don.

"Affirmative," Don responded.

"We'll be there, sir."

"Text me the details so I can start work on it."

As they prepared to leave, Don called Efe, who had left early to attend to some businesses, informing him of the quick trip. Also, he called Queen to tell her he would be back before nightfall. He was discreet, though, with his conversation with her, avoiding suspicion with the boys. Banji drove them to the airport in 50 minutes. On their way, Ace boasted of how he was favored during his training and how he had met with top-ranking officers. He spoke about his value and how he was offered a very high-paying job compared to his peers.

Bala had picked up the case file and studied it before they arrived. It was obvious that the suspect was ignorant of the law; he wouldn't have been locked up for so long without being granted bail or charged to court. He was very excited to see Ace and repeatedly called him *bad boy*, shaking and tapping him on the shoulder. They did some catching up, and he deliberately ignored Don. Ace was caught between not offending his superior and leaving Don unacknowledged. He finally found a safe moment to introduce the two of them, and they briefly exchanged pleasantries.

Bala, a tall, broad-chested dark guy in his early forties, was formerly a police officer. He was drafted into the force three years earlier on the instructions of the former director. He was very articulate and confronting and was well-known for his fearless audacity when handling top politicians with high-profile cases. He once studied in the U.K., hence his feigned British accent that was clouded by his deep Hausa diction.

He asked them to wait at the lobby while he issued certain instructions to four waiting junior officers. Afterwards, he asked the two visitors to follow him to his office. They climbed two flights of stairs and walked the long hallway to the last room on the right. He motioned Don to sit on the waiting bench and took Ace with him. The field office had four desks, one each for the four occupying officers, and a chest of drawers.

Bala introduced Ace to his colleagues and boasted about his protégé; apparently he had told them about him before he came. They welcomed him with little jokes and laughed. Don cursed under his breath for being so belittled.

"Down to business, Dayo, I have studied this case but I know there's more to it than what has been documented. You will give me every detail there is, I will get your brother out on bail tomorrow and he will be a totally free man in two weeks, Insha Allah. One more thing, have you told the man outside that he will be paying us 30 percent of the money before anything is done?"

"He's aware of that," Ace answered.

"Good... now tell me."

"The suspect conned a businessman into investing in oil smuggling. He paid the money on the belief that he would get a supply of diesel worth six times his capital. The man outside had persuaded him to accept half of the money and let the suspect off the hook, but he would not oblige," Ace explained.

"End of story, the case is solved already. I will invite the complainant to my office for an interview. I will highlight his greed and threaten that his entire business enterprise is under investigation. He will have no choice but to back down since his venture with the suspect is illegal."

They talked further and both went out to meet Don. He instructed Don to make a payment of 9 million to Ace and expect his brother at home the next day. He also promised that the case would be totally struck out in two weeks. He had told Ace to deduct 3 million and credit a discreet account with 6 million on his behalf.

When Ace got the money, he gave Banji a million naira cut. Bala did as he promised.

CHAPTER 11

Queen had been in Don's house some three weeks; he had enjoyed every bit of it. He had been very much in need of a Nigerian wife, but no girl made sense to him as much as she did. He had tried tirelessly to date her, but she had always avoided him. On the day they first met, a friend of Queen's had called her, informing her of some rich guys that needed escorts for the night. They had a great time at the club, and the conversation was really deep. They had a lot to drink, and she gave him the best mouth job he had ever had, en-route to the hotel room. The sex had been one of a kind, too.

In his house, she had begun to fill a big vacuum and had been very supportive in his business. Her scam knowledge had also been a plus as she had been able to add some input to the daily running of the company. She woke up early every morning to exercise in Don's private gym and also jog around the house. She then swam in the large swimming pool for an hour. It was paradise for her, but she had to act the part. Afterwards she prepared Don's breakfast. They spent most of each day together, except on occasion when Don had to go to town for meetings or when she had to buy fresh groceries. One sunny afternoon, Don came home with a shiny Mini Cooper he bought from a friend's car lot. Queen was moved, really happy and could hardly hold back her joy. She kissed him passionately in the presence of the boys. She was barely seen, since she mostly locked herself in Don's private quarters. It was the best gift she'd ever had. Too excited, she called her mom to inform her and had to confess she wasn't in school but in Benin.

After three days of driving lessons, she became bold enough to ride into town on her own. The new car also prompted her to frequent the market. There was always something to buy, and Sophie became her ride buddy. Sophie and Queen had bonded really well over the weeks. Queen had tried hard to help Sophie with her self-esteem issues. She always reminded Sophie how beautiful she was in her plus size and how African men loved big bosoms. They even strategized on how to get her married quickly. With Queen, Sophie began kitchen lesson 101 and in a week, she prepared her first meal for the house. Everyone was thrilled and happy with her evolving domestication.

All the boys crushed on Queen in their closet and ended it there. She was too beautiful to behold, some of them confessed, and the fear of the Don also crippled their fantasy. Vitali was her biggest fan; he created false reasons to see the Don in his quarters.

He believed he would make a better suitor judging by his physique. To him, Queen didn't deserve to be with a criminal like Don.

The Queen had proved to be a really nice matron, her smile readily available to anyone she came in contact with. She also interceded on their behalf with her boyfriend. Once in a while, she cooked large meals for the entire house and personally supervised the house inventory and cleaning. With all her input and the obvious change she brought to the mansion, she managed to maintain her seclusion. She had become friends with a movie bootlegger in town who supplied her with fresh releases every other day. She and her boyfriend spent their days watching them; Don, who barely watched TV, then spent most of his time doing the unusual. Each time he decided to watch news or boring stuff, he made use of other screens, as Queen could not be disturbed.

Don had gone away on a quick business trip. These two days seemed to Queen like weeks. She realized she had become very fond of him and missed him very much. They talked on the phone to bridge the distance. As she swam in the pool one fine Sunday morning, it dawned on her that she had drifted from her set goals. She had vowed not to depend on men financially and to become rich on her own. Don's generosity and promise of a good life wasn't guaranteed.

She knew by experience that the time she was spending in his house was just a few weeks of honeymoon and that the mood would change shortly.

Besides, Benin was not the place for her. She couldn't imagine living in the quiet town, and worst of all, Don would not live anywhere else in the country, not even for her. She finally decided to return to her hustle, taking advantage of the luxury of time and the comfort of the house.

She returned to her quarters, took a cold shower, dried her hot body and put on a shower robe. She then moved to the store and selected a brand new MacBook from the stack of laptops. She removed the sleek machine from its carton, walked to the main dining area and placed it on the table. She called one of the boys on the intercom; three of them showed up with a quarter-empty bottle of Jack Daniels. They were drinking when she called. They offered her a glass, but she politely turned it down. While she told them what she needed on the computer, they got into a conversation and in a few minutes the whole house was present in the room. They had never been able to talk this much with Queen, and they concluded that she was actually not bad. They lured her into cooking one of her many great dishes, and she agreed.

Sophie screamed, "Let's throw a party!"

All concurred. There hadn't been one since the house was launched; Don never celebrated anything. A convoy of four cars left for town, led by Queen's car. She broke off the chain and headed for the local market, where she and Sophie bought groceries. Vitali and two other guys drove to the biggest liquor store in town and loaded his SUV with drinks. The third car went to pick up the D.J. and the fourth, to inform close friends who couldn't be reached by phone – University of Benin girls especially.

By 5 p.m. the poolside was filled with party people, girls in their bikinis and guys in boxer shorts. There was plenty to drink and eat, and there was barbeque, too. Don arrived minutes past eight, frowning. He hated having people loiter in his house, and of course his consent wasn't sought. Queen had called him to come home urgently; he thought there was an emergency. He was going to yell at everyone, but the Queen's welcome gesture changed his mind. She raced to him with her drop-dead gorgeous, fair-skinned body in a caramel-colored bikini that blended with her complexion, making her seem like she wasn't wearing anything; faint drops of chlorinated water were still on her body from the swimming pool. In her palms were a bottle of champagne and two glasses, and she was wearing the smile she wore when she was drilling him in the bedroom.

She's the best thing to ever happen to me, he thought to himself as he grabbed her wholly.

The mix of chlorine, her body scent and the fullness of her cleavage sent shivers up his spine. He became more aroused the moment their lips met. They kissed. The suddenness of the scenario and velocity of Queen's motion sent the duo falling on the handsomely-manicured lawn like kids, neither mouth leaving the other. The partying crowd yelled with excitement and admiration as they took pictures with their phones. The D.J. changed the tempo to a more suitable song. The Don and Queen soon realized all eyes were on them and slowly attempted to sit up.

One of Queen's tits slipped out of her swim gear, exposing a lighter skin and a very dark, pointing nipple. She hurriedly grabbed Don and fixed herself under the shield of his body. Sophie rushed to them and wrapped her in a towel.

"My boss and his wife sure know how to make a good movie," she said very audibly, and the crowd cheered with laughter. The two lovers rose to their feet, picked up the champagne, the glasses and Don's iPad and walked slowly into the house amidst applause and cheering.

They were barely into the bedroom before they resumed kissing safe from prying eyes. Their passion was too intense; the wildcat in Queen evolved from its forever slumber and dominated her like a dreaded alter ego. A little fear gripped Don at the force behind the push into the large bed. He barely made the bed from the distance of the push. He was glad the whole of his torso made it at least.

Queen crawled in between his legs and loosened his belt, pulling it out of its straps and throwing it into oblivion. All these she did at a pace that surprised Don. She unbuttoned his white linen pants and tried to unzip them, but her impatience made the zipper lock in defiance to her demand. Don attempted to sit up and work the zipper, but she pushed him back into place. She pinched a little portion of the pants five inches away from the hard zipper and dipped her incisors into it, ripping the length of his right thigh from the linen all at once. From his lying position, staring far into the big star engraved on Plaster of Paris ceiling, he wore a mischievous smile.

This is her majesty at her best. He concluded.

Now having enough access to his underneath, she pulled out his manhood from his boxer briefs and swallowed the girth, filling her mouth to her guts. Then, she worked it with the dexterity inspired by her intoxication. Four minutes into the show, with the Don already in a state and groaning with pleasure, the single star right above him turned into a galaxy of stars as he saw himself soaring in galactic fantasy. He shrieked loudly, placed his left hand on her head, stroking her hair and pulling it with a firm subtle grip. At that point, she knew he was going to cum in another minute and kill her fire. She stopped, stood to her feet, ripping her bikini while at it. She motioned Don to move into the center of the bed facing up, but he decided to take charge this time.

He got off the bed, motioning her into a doggie position while she held the tip of the bed. He held her by the hip with his left hand; grabbing his rock-solid dick with the right, he tapped her soft behind with it a couple of times like a baton…what he does to withhold ejaculation. He then thrust his mass into her warm, juicy inner, causing her to gasp for air. They spent the next half hour murdering each other with passion.

The next afternoon, she received her well-furnished laptop and flirted with it in much excitement, taking her time to refresh from the last time she was online. She went through her email to recover all her phony details and saved her most needed files on the desktop. Queen and Don had returned to the party the previous night shortly after the mind-blowing round of hot sex. They had mingled with the guests for half an hour and had returned to their quarters to sleep.

She woke up very early to supervise the cleaning of the yard and had her regular morning drills. After breakfast, she and Don had watched a romantic movie that he bought on iTunes. It amused her that he could be so thoughtful, and she remained sweet most of the day. With her brand-new tool, she was ready to face the world, believing that the sleekness of the machine would bring her good luck. She had a strong determination not to be distracted by anything until she laid her hands on a duffle bag full of money. While romancing the computer and dreaming, Don walked into the dining area.

"I see you got yourself a new laptop. What's the plan?"

"I'm going to make me a minimum of $50,000 before the end of the year," she declared.

Don chuckled, "How are you going to achieve that?" he asked.

"The way everybody does."

"With me, you'll lack nothing. I'll give you everything you need… just name it," he said, patronizing her.

"I know, babe, it's not what you think. You're a very kind man, and I know you'll do what's best for me, but believe me, this is just principle, and I've made up my mind. Watch this space," she said with a wink.

Feeling defeated, he agreed, but with an ulterior belief that she'd get tired in her first two days.

"OK, honey, do what you have to do. I got your back if you need me," he said, kissed her on the cheek and walked away.

***

She never got tired. One week later she was waxing strong. She had made $200 in four days but lost the client a couple of hours later. She was really happy, not for the amount she made but for the fact that she had broken a jinx. It was proof to her that she could make money from dating scams. She also started to get much more comfortable at Don's house, believing it was surrounded by a good omen. This thinking wasn't exclusive to her alone; every rookie in this game attached a lot of superstition to success or failure. It was believed that if you try for long and you don't make some money, regardless of how little it may be, it was a waste of time. Some don't give up, no matter what. They strived for close to two years, believing their luck would shine someday. It actually did shine... over time they mastered the art, corrected their errors and ended up making big hits.

With this money, she cooked a rare dish that was considered to be a royal meal for the house. Everyone knew the Queen had made her first money, and it was just right for her to host her friends. They celebrated with her and promised to be of assistance should she need any. Some of them talked about their first major hits and how they had lived wasteful lives; a couple of them confessed to still live such lives. They talked about how they met Don and how he changed their lives. Vitali's story stood out as the most remarkable. Don made jest of all of them, indicating their flaws and weaknesses.

He was hardly this accessible, and they all laughed at his sarcasm. The meal was tagged "SOUL FOOD" and it registered perfectly. The large table had a cluster of big earthen pots, each filled with varieties such as vegetable soup with periwinkles, fried snails, goat-head pepper soup, smoked catfish, pounded yam and plenty of red wine.

***

Unperturbed with the loss of the client who paid her and blocked her hours later, she worked on the others she met on the same site. A short while later, they noticed her scam profile. She lost them, too. She buzzed her scammer friends on Yahoo Messenger asking them about the sites they were working on then. She brainstormed with one of them on whether free sites or paid sites had most potential for clients who would pay. She concluded from the discussion that she could find clients from wherever. There was no point following the crowd, finding clients from sites that ban you at every sniff of scam, especially sites that every scammer she knew was using.

She decided to take her time researching and strategizing. She visited scam-combating sites to read reviews of common scams and comments made on such forums. She read stories of scam victims, how they met con artists, how they were fooled by promises of love, how they still believed the person they spoke with really existed and all. How some have exposed their nudity through webcams, never seeing the other party on cam even once. She read stories of some who sold their properties and some who jettisoned their ward's college funds to pay for their lover's expensive adventurous hobbies. She made notes on her desktop from her wide reading. She scoured popular sites, studying their registration processes, total number of members, number of members per country, race, success stories, scam campaigns and adopted programs. She studied so much that she could tell a good dating site from the texture of its website. Now ready with her own ideas after spending several hours at the computer, she decided to take a break for the day.

Next morning, she searched for her own choice of dating site, one that catered to the personality she had built for herself and the type of clients she hoped to meet. She eventually decided to register on *www. collegegradlove.com.* A site popular among college graduates, it encouraged users to search its database for friends they had crushes on in their college days. It also automatically matched users based on the extracurricular activities they were involved in school, non-academic interests such as sports, drama, music, hunting, gambling and more. It sort of had a list of everyone that went to college in the United States, with updated marital info.

She Googled for a name with a matching African American face, a tiring process. It took her three days to find the right person, and when she finally did, she looked her up on all available social networks, stealing as many pictures as possible. She sent a passport-sized photo to one of the guys who made her a driver's license and a travel passport. She also got a United States phone number and recorded a voice note on its voicemail service. She did everything she could think of and perfected her storyline and all the tools she would be using. With everything ready, she signed up at the dating site, inputting all the data she had gathered, and created an attractive profile for herself. Using blockers, she prevented the kind of people she wouldn't want to buzz her and highlighted those she had interests in, mainly high-income earners.

Soon she began to receive emails and flirts. So many of them came that she had to shortlist who to chat and communicate with. She somehow had a strong feeling she was on a really good site and got highly convinced she will do well in there.

CHAPTER 12

Somewhere in the Emirates, 26-year-old Waheed Ibn Ahmad was sitting quietly in his office. He reclined his chair, reminiscing. Waheed was the son of a wealthy Emirati oil merchant. He was worth $26 million. From his large rectangular office, he could see the world around him. It was situated on the 52nd floor of a high-rise in Abu Dhabi. From his desk, there was hardly anything he needed in the world that he couldn't get. He only needed to make one phone call, and it was done.

He'd recently struck a major deal for his father's company, acquiring a dying shipping line for their export business. The purchase was a tough one; the shipping firm had a lot of vessels in its name, but the owners were retiring. There were a lot of competitors in the bid, and it almost seemed he was going to lose the deal. It was his first major assignment unaccompanied, and the challenge was cutthroat. Dressed in his white Kaftan and turban, he stood in the large conference room amidst old businessmen the age of his father and older. His little speech on how much he loved boats, how he was able to salvage his uncle's Duretti in mid-sea when he was 13, saving eight lives including his own, had touched the heart of the CEO's wife, who was the CFO of the company. The boyish innocence, coupled with his obvious passion for boats, his position of high responsibility and his respect for the elderly, all won him the deal, although his bid was fourth on the list.

The CFO had said, "This young man will definitely care for our boats better than we did and obviously better than anyone in this room. He is not buying these boats for just business. He is going to love them and take care of them. He is the youngest in this meeting and he has many decades ahead of him," she cracked a little joke.

"We barely have any left," they all laughed and applauded her. The husband, seeing the direction she was heading, had tried to signal her to stop, seeing they had the opportunity of making more money if they sold to the highest bidder, but she ignored him.

"Our company will be sold to this fine young man who has a lot of future ahead of him, and we will put in our best to guide and support him in any way we can. Thank you, gentlemen, my husband and I are honored to be seated among you today. We hope to meet again."

A big applause ensued after her speech, and everyone stood to congratulate the young Arab who was wearing a big shy smile. When the prospective buyers had left, the old lady had called Waheed to her side and whispered in his ear, "You will assist us in buying a home on one of those islands; Jerry and I will retire there. He may die if he doesn't see those boats often; besides, you need a lot of his advice, and I don't want to be a widow right yet."

"That's a good one, ma'am. I'm very grateful for your support," he'd replied. "I will make sure that you get everything you need, Insha Allah."

Waheed had been match-made with a lot of beautiful women. His family and relatives relentlessly invited him to parties and functions, which he barely acknowledged. At the few that he attended, he barely mingled. He missed the U.S., the wild party life and the girls. He would rather have remained there after school and worked like everyone does. He yearned for the free life, one that was not governed by convention, one away from his protective parents.

He was born wealthy, the last and only male child of his parents, his mother's beloved and his father's best friend. He was the best thing to happen to them. Playful and adventurous when he was a kid, he had grown up into a fine young man, tall, lanky, fair-skinned and very attractive. He would pass for a successful model. He spent a lot of his holidays with his dad's younger brother while growing up, a happy-go-lucky marine biologist and an adrenaline junkie. They would scuba-dive for hours in search of rare marine life, the reefs of Dubai being their best spot. Waheed found an ancient golden dagger in the reefs. It made him believe it was bestowed with lost treasure.

After many years of fruitless search, he finally gave in but safely kept his discovery with his mother.

There were times they went shark-tagging in the open seas. They were exhilarating moments. He still got to do that when very tempted but he'd had a fill to last a lifetime. The memory of his friend's recklessness still haunted him; he had vowed never to do it again with a rookie. There were five sharks swimming within a perimeter of 300 square meters. The ocean was calm and beautifully blue. The open marine habitation, dotted with young leisurely-swimming sharks, was a scene to relish for the biologist. He would spend hours in such splendor, savoring the wonders of nature and the gentility with which the dreaded beasts maneuvered in their haven, not minding human intrusion and touch.

The obstinate teenager was instructed to remain in the cage while Waheed and his uncle swam with the sharks; his dying desire to touch a live shark saw the better of him. He unlocked the cage and swam freely in the shark-infested waters. Not heeding the warnings of the two pros, he touched a two-year-old baby wrongly; it got really angry and swam off furiously. Twenty feet away, it turned back and headed towards him. Waheed and his uncle, foreseeing what would happen, left their pleasure swim and made daring darts towards him. They would have been a little too late, but the shark was able to devour a pound of flesh from Hammed's butt. Suddenly the calm blue revealed small maps of red from his injury; this aroused the other sharks. In a split second, a number of sharks came raging towards them. They were fortunate enough to make it into the small cage and they bolted themselves in.

Many years later, they would joke about the incident, laughing hysterically. But it hurt Waheed that his wild moments were numbered. He was given strict instructions and was usually monitored whenever he visited his uncle. He wasn't allowed beyond the shores of the gulf nation. Apparently, his parents were not aware of his escapades; their belief was that he never swam beyond the reefs.

***

These days, he was occupied with piles of work. He controlled a large chunk of his father's estate, knowing there was no room for mistakes. Since his successful acquisition of the shipping company, he had become the face of the various companies. At his very young age, he was saddled with so much responsibility that only his tactful mind and split-second decisions could handle. He inherited managerial skills not from his father but from his mother, a linguist who had never worked in official capacity but had been the bedrock of the family: a kind-hearted woman who was never prejudiced by religion or culture, even though she was a devout Muslim. A contemporary mother she was called by her children; she had enjoyed seeing her children grow into the adults they wished to be but with strict guidance of the teachings of the Quran. As for their father, tough decisions he couldn't make on his own at work, situations that confused him, were solved at dinner in the presence of the children.

He was never carried away with the ego of his peer or the cockiness of success. He loved his wife and allowed the family to bond into a harmonious entity. Now that their two daughters were married, Waheed, being a young adult, kept late nights or locked himself up in his chalet. Those good moments were only spoken about these days, except for days when the grandchildren came visiting. Waheed studied Economics at the University of Massachusetts. He kept a low profile and had only two close friends. Although his account always had a minimum of 800,000 dollars on his mother's insistence, he never exhibited the traits of wealth. He lived life like a regular and was very studious.

One day, while running an errand for his dad, he flew economy from Boston to Miami.

"13C, 13C, 13C," the fair-skinned African American girl with dreadlocks kept whispering, like she was reciting a rhyme as she came jostling in. He didn't notice her walk down the cabin until he heard the faint number a row away. He looked up to behold the most sensual woman he had ever seen; he couldn't get his eyes off her and he was caught in her web. He motioned her to the seat beside him – he couldn't utter a word but made directions with his hand.

"Thank you!" she said. Those were the words that broke his hypnosis. He quietly picked up his journal, pretending to be going through his notes. "Are you going to ignore me cos I got dreadlocks or something?" she asked with sarcastic cynicism.

He smiled back at her sheepishly and stuttered slowly, "You're the most beautiful girl in the world."

She went mushy, holding both hands to her chest saying, "Aww, that's so sweet. No one has said that to me in a long, long time… thank you."

"You're welcome," he said and went back to his notes.

"You haven't told me what you're going to do at the beaches… I'm going swimming. You can join me… I'm unaccompanied."

"I'm going to take delivery of a boat," he responded, still pretending to be engrossed in his note.

"Are you a deckhand or do you work with a boat builder?"

"I'm picking up my mother's yacht and sailing with it to Dubai."

"Now you are kidding me. You own a ship and you fly economy? Thank you so much, sir. It was nice meeting you. Ciao!" she said, adjusting herself in her seat. She buckled her seatbelt and fumbled with her iPod.

"I'm very serious," he said with some effort to convince her. "You're welcome aboard to inspect it. She's very beautiful. My father built it especially for my mom; her 50th birthday is in a few weeks, and the boat bears her name."

She ignored him, and they didn't say a word until the plane landed. She came out to the arrivals before him and waited. He could see her more clearly now in the open; she looked a lot more beautiful in her leggings, miniskirt and leather jacket. She stood tall in her wedge shoes and her skinny long legs. She was traveling light; she had only a big handbag tucked on her right arm. The other hand she folded into a fist that she rested on her waist. She tilted her head to the right as if she didn't notice him coming.

As he got next to her, not allowing him to say a word, she said, "You're going to show me this boat or its goodbye forever!"

"OK."

He hailed a cab, and they drove the distance between the airport and the dockyard, not saying a word. He tried to utter something, but she shut him up by showing him her left palm and facing her right, as she looked into the roads. They finally arrived at the yard that spanned three acres with large structures that looked like airplane hangars. They walked to the business office, and on opening the door, a nicely-dressed man in a grey suit spotted Waheed and paced hurriedly towards them both, smiling from ear to ear.

"Mr. Ahmad, it's so good to see you. I've been expecting you. I must tell you that you will be impressed at the final touches we have given to your boat. Your boat now looks like a vessel made in heaven. I personally saw to its finishing," the college-trained salesman said, shaking hands with Waheed.

"OK," was all that Waheed said. He was a bit timid because of his guest; he didn't want to seem pompous. The salesman exchanged pleasantries with the lady, and they shook hands.

"I should take you to your boat; it's been docked and ready to go," the salesman said, expecting to see the boat-buyer as excited as he had been each time he came to see the work in progress. He was confused about his acquaintance but he simply did his work.

He walked them to a waiting Range Rover that drove them for some three minutes to where the boat was berthed. The appearance of the large luxury vessel, a hundred yards from where they were parked, was overwhelming, as the afternoon sunlight amply bathed the magnificent white monster in golden yellow. The immaculate white hull stood thirty feet above sea level, commanding respect from boats nearby. It stood tall and majestic, a promise of royal ownership.

The dreadlocked girl stood dumbfounded at the size of the boat; she didn't leave the side of the SUV. The salesman had dragged Waheed towards the boat, not pausing once in his talk. When they were on the deck, Waheed noticed his friend was not with them. He walked to the front deck and signaled her to join them. She walked over and joined them on the deck. She excused the boat-buyer from the salesman and dragged him to a nearby compartment, holding his arm.

With the warm afternoon breeze blowing cool moisture to her face, she said, "I'm so sorry for the disrespect, Mister. You don't get to meet yacht owners every day, especially in economy class. Anyway, I'm Tatyana. It is so nice to meet you. I'll be leaving and I hope you enjoy the beautiful boat," and started walking away.

"I thought you were unaccompanied," he said to her, raising a hand to block the sunlight from his eyes.

She stood still, not turning around; she tilted her face back to look at him and said, "Yes I am."

"I might be needing an assistant captain," he said a little louder.

She smiled, walked back to him and raised her hand in salute. "Aye aye, sir!"

They spent the next four days inspecting the boat and preparing for the long sail. They spent some time on the beach, too, went clubbing and got drenched in alcohol. They spent the nights on the boat sleeping only in his room. Some hours in the day, they spent sunbathing on the wide deck of the boat. The remainder of their time was spent painting the beach city red. The very conservative Arab bloke kept swiping his platinum card at every shop they visited. They stocked fine champagne, liquor, cigarettes; Tatyana made sure they got weed.

A day before they were to leave, the boat builders mandated that they sailed with two deckhands, even though Waheed declined the complementary delivery by an experienced crew. He strongly wanted to sail the boat alone. They sensed what the couple had in mind and promised the deckhands would be out of sight as much as possible. Waheed summoned the two assistants to the boat like he was going to have serious talks with them. They ended up getting blown on weed. He asked them to find themselves a girl each from the beach who would sail with them on his bill; they were really happy and they thanked him too much.

They spent the next 18 days on the oceans having the time of their lives. Waheed and Tatyana didn't realize the true beauty of the boat until they lived in it. There was a new discovery everyday as they sailed.

Waheed often swam in the endless waters, but the others were satisfied with the swimming pool on the deck. A day before they arrived in Dubai, they all embarked on extensive cleaning, whitewashing all the parts of the boat that they had used. He paid the two Miami girls $3,000 each and dropped them off before they arrived.

***

His father had promised to take his mom on a friend's boat for two days to celebrate her birthday. The plan got her excited, and she prayed a whole month that she'd see the light of that day. She did enjoy those moments; they were the best two days of her life. According to plan, Waheed had picked the families of his two older sisters, relatives and friends from another dock and sailed to an empty dock where his parents would get disappointed. They had turned back to leave, his mother wrapped in his father's consoling arms, when a sudden continuous loud blaring honk filled the shoreline. They paused and turned around. She went weak in his firm grip and almost dropped to her knees when she saw the bold calligraphy written in gold-plated metal bearing *"NURA HABIBI"* on the enormous boat. It was practically placed by the boat's hull close to its toe-rail.

She remained weak and could barely stand on her own. The staffers who carried their boxes had to fetch something from nowhere for her to sit on. By the time the boat had berthed properly, Waheed raced to join his father to lead her onto the boat, but she had regained her strength. She continuously hit her son with her purse, accusing him of conspiring with his father. He kept running back and forth as she chased him tirelessly. Her husband walked at his own pace, laughing. He clapped his hands each time she hit him with the purse. They eventually climbed onto the boat.

Their son, the captain, by virtue of his duty, took it upon himself to introduce them to the boat and show them around. He described the facilities on the boat's deck. He boasted of how he had sourced the best possible builder and how the company had invested its best craftsmanship into the construction. He told them that he would be delighted to show them around, but it would only be proper that he showed them what laid within, especially their bedroom. They were delighted.

He opened the big gold-framed tinted glass doors to a cheering crowd that kept screaming happy birthday.

CHAPTER 13

The Queen had responded to the several emails she received on the dating site. She had chatted endlessly with some of her prospects, too, and she was doing it pretty well. Her concentration on her new job had created a little gap between her and Don, which made him not so cool with it. He complained about her being too engrossed on scams rather than being the woman of the house or willing to start up a business that he will finance. They argued over this often, but she usually had her way with him.

One day, she received an email from Abu Dhabi, from a profile named 'BOATGUY.'

Hi, you look just like the woman I used to love. Can we chat sometime?

She went through his profile, screening every available detail. The guy was young, obviously rich based on his nationality and job description, although he didn't include details of his income. He was good-looking and classy, too, from his pictures on a big yacht.

She responded:

Sure, butterflyjennylove@yahoo.com

Twelve minutes later, she received an add request and accepted it. A chat ensued immediately.

Boatman:

Hey!

Butterflies:

Hey

Boatman:

Nice profile u got there, u're very beautiful *smile*

Butterflies:

Thank you

Boatman:

Tell me more

Butterflies:

What u wanna know?

Boatman:

How are your folks?

Noticing he couldn't pick a good conversation, she decides to help.

Butterflies:

They good, mom annoyed me today…she's 2 much in my business *sad*

Boatman:

Lol, dat's what parents are there 4, I'm sure she wants d best for you

Butterflies:

I know, I love her wit all my heart but she's a lot of pain lately *angry*

She says I study 2 hard, work 2 much, blablabla

I don't have room for romance and all

Boatman:

I can imagine

You should relax a lil…my recommendation

Butterflies:

Tnx, I try when I can…I love my work

Boatman:

I'm glad you do, nothin better than doin what you love

I won't trade mine for anything *biggrin*

Butterflies:

What do you do

Boatman:

I'm a drug dealer *coolface*

Butterflies:

Funny

Boatman:

I manage my dad's business *nerd*

Butterflies:

He must be rich *wink*

Boatman:

He's just a regular guy…we service boats and also do small jobs for oil companies

All their dirty work like cleaning jobs, laundry for staff and all those lil things they won't bother with

Butterflies:

Lol, u make it sound like menial work, that's contract work dude!

Owning a boat is an expensive hobby too, your customers will pay good money for your services

Boatman:

They try *biggrin*

Butterflies:

I envy u…u make my job sound boring

I luv it tho but I'll prefer boatwork better, with that I can sail often *wink*

Boatman:

I can hire u if u don't cost too much

Butterflies:

I'm expensive…very expensive!

Boatman:

I'll go bankrupt *laugh*

Butterflies:

Lol… what are your hobbies

Boatman:

Hmm…marine is my life

I love scuba diving, hunting, camel racing in the desert and I love drag racing

I also love music and movies too *wink*

She leans back on her chair, her jaw in her hand, wearing a confused face.

Butterflies:

Whats scuba diving

Boatman:

Swimming in the ocean with all those kits dat u see in documentaries.

Butterflies:

Oh, I get what u mean now…must be fun

U should teach me someday…hopefully.

Boatman:

I'll be pleased!

Butterflies:

Great! I love music too…what girl doesn't love the movies, I love to swim and drive and cook

The list is endless

Boatman:

In my culture, a girl must know how to cook

Butterflies:

Every woman shud knw how to cook regardless of culture, I learnt from my mom

Boatman:

Lucky u, it's not compulsory in your country

I used to date a girl that looks very much like u, she's as beautiful as u

She was a really good cook too, we once sailed from miami to Dubai delivering a boat together…it was fun…we fed on seafood mostly

I would swim in the ocean in boxers to catch strange fish and crustaceans

Butterflies:

Wow! *surprised*

Glad ur alive

Boatman:

Lol there was a lot to drink too, we were like pirates drinking rum *biggrin*

Butterflies:

I love to swim but I wont go in the ocean…I wont sail that far either

Boatman:

I'll help you through it

Butterflies:

U guys must have had too much sex *smh*

He pauses for a second and stares into space, wearing a mischievous smile.

Boatman:

You can say that again *biggrin* *wink*

Butterflies:

Since u had much fun together, y r u not together anymo

Boatman:

Her ex-boyfriend was a club bouncer and former boxer...he punched me once in the tummy and warned me never to see her again *itwasntme*

She laughed so much that she fell off her chair; Sophie heard her laughing and rushed to meet her from where she sat reading a book. She asked, "What's going on, Queen?"

"There's this maga I'm chatting with, he's very funny. He was beaten cos of a girl," she said.

Sophie responded, standing behind her and reading the chat, "Now that's funny. And he's open about it?"

"He's 26, and I sense he's playful."

"Good for you. I hope he has money?" Sophie asked.

"I'm sure he does."

Butterflies:

rollingonthefloorlaugh *rollingonthefloorlaugh* *rollingonthefloorlaugh*

I just fell off the chair laughing

He turned his chair around and laughed, too. "This girl is funny," he said.

Butterflies:

I dont hav an ex that beats people *wink*
Boatman:
I'm glad you don't
Are you working today?
Butterflies:
Lazy day today, I'm on study leave
Boatman:
Bookworm
Butterflies:
Thank u…boatboy *tongueout*
Boatman:
Hehehe
I have to go for now, will chat with you later at
night if you're online
Got to attend to some boats right now *wink*
Butterflies:
Cool!
Enjoy…
Boatman:
It was nice meeting you jenny
Butterflies:
Same here
Boatman:
kiss *kiss*
Butterflies:
smile

He went back to work, smiling. She stepped away from her laptop, stretching. She walked out into the yard to meet Sophie, who was smoking weed at the poolside with Vitali and two other guys. She talked with them for a minute and entered her quarters. Don was seated on the bed playing FIFA 13 on the PS3. She sat behind him, wrapping her arms round his stomach.

"It's sunny outside, let's go swimming," she invited him.

Don replied, "Are you done with your work?"

"For now, yes. I met this funny Arab guy; he told me how his ex's ex-boyfriend beat him up."

"For real?" Don asked, chuckling, still engrossed in his game.

"Let's go swimming, babe," she pressed, dragging the pad with him. "You haven't swam in ages."

"OK… OK, I'm almost done, gimme one minute, I'm almost done. Get prepared," he said, still playing the game.

"Hmmm," she said, with a mischievous look on her face; she got off the bed and walked around him to stand between him and the screen. She strip-danced for him, ripping off her clothes one by one, seducing him. As she gradually went topless, she cupped her tits in her hands, whining to his face. He tried to grab her, but she retreated. Still in her belly-dancing mode, she pulled off her joggers and threw them at him. Don rose to his feet and launched to catch her. Knowing what he was about to do, she broke off, running. He followed, and they chased each other around the big room. She got exhausted and tried to hide behind the curtains; he grabbed her and carried her, throwing her into the waiting bed.

They didn't swim anymore; they passed out from exhaustion. Three hours later, she prepared a light dinner with fruits and fetched her laptop. She responded to emails and browsed through profiles on the site. Don joined her, and they both pondered over ideas. He taught her how to find and notice successful clients. He looked up Waheed's profile, too, and browsed through their conversation.

"Tag well with this one, he smells like good money. Every UAE citizen is wealthy. When you are done getting all you can from him, we'll visit him and suck him of all he's got."

"I'll put my back into it, sir!" she said with great enthusiasm. He lay down facing the ceiling; she laid her head on his torso looking into his face.

"What will my cut be?"

"Mad sex," he answered, chuckling.

"In your mind," she said, pouting. "Be serious, young man... this is business!"

"Job owners usually get 30 percent. That's what you'll be getting, too. You never know, he may cough out a million dollars," Don says with a phony smile.

"With my cut, I'll buy my parents a new home. I will travel the world and buy the best shoes there possibly could be."

"Good idea, Queen."

They heard messenger alerts, and she went back to work.

Boatman:
Hey
Pretty you there
Butterflies:
*I'm here hun...miss me already? *wink**

Boatman:

Sorta

Butterflies:

Not good enough *talktothehand*

Boatman:

Of course I miss you *kiss* *kiss*

Butterflies:

Good boy

Mama is going to teach u some manners

How to treat a lady right

Boatman:

Yes ma'am

Butterflies:

How was ur work with the boats

Boatman:

Successful… Alhamdulilah

Butterflies:

Good good

Had something to eat?

Boatman:

Naaa…food is not my thing

Butterflies:

You should eat and have some skin

I like 2 hav something to hold onto in my man….
dont like too much bones *wink*

Boatman:

Cool ma'am…for you I'll add some flesh

Butterflies:

I have this thing for obedient bois… I'm liking u
already

Boatman:

Yaay! *party* When are you visiting
Butterflies:
Just like dat…I barely knw u
Boatman:
We're building up
Butterflies:
We need 2 take it slow…lets knw each other better
Boatman:
I love speed *biggrin*
Butterflies:
I'm a granny, I drive slow *tongueout*
Boatman:
We'll get there…by air or by carriage lol
Butterflies:
Lol
Boatman:
You have study holiday…you can read in Abu Dhabi, I'll hire a professor to help you with your studying
Butterflies:
Where's a boatboy goin 2 get such money from
Boatman:
Won't cost notin…anything you want, I'll do for you
DING!!!

Excited, Queen jumped to her feet on the bed and did ballet on the soft foam, walking over a smiling Don. "I've hit the jackpot," she said loudly.

"Take it easy, Queen; you need to take your time. Obviously he's a good catch, but you can also lose him if you play it wrong," Don advised her after reading her last chats. "You need to get back to work… you don't want to keep him waiting."

She returned to her laptop.

Butterflies:

*Tempting… but I'll just do the reading myself…
you can come over to California…we can have coffee
at a nice café*

We can talk and take it from there

If u make me laugh… I might just touch ur face

*I may as well peck u on the cheek…or on ur lips
*wink**

Boatman:

Hmm *thinking*

Butterflies:

*U may end up driving me to San Francisco and
unto ur errand boat *wink**

wink

Don, who had been reading, smiled, staring at
her.

"You are brilliant," he told her graciously. He
meant it.

"I learn from the best," she acknowledged with a
broad smile.

Boatman:

*The boat will be a good idea *daydreaming*
*lovestruck**

Butterflies:

Come and get it *eyelashes*

Boatman:

*Will work somethin out, not in the next month…
can't leave Abu Dhabi for more than 24 hrs right now*

I work round the clock

Butterflies:

Take ur time romeo…we got plenty of time
Boatman:
True true but I need u now
Butterflies:
What time is it over there
Boatman:
10.17pm Wednesday
Butterflies:
Wow!! u live on the otherside of the world…its 10.19am
Boatman:
Time zone things…hope that wont bother our chats *sad*
Butterflies:
Of course not, I'm available round the clock too *biggrin*
Boatman:
Awesome!

They chatted a little longer and ended the conversation. She drifted into sleep afterward, wrapped in Don's arms.

***

1 a.m. Nigerian time, she awoke to attend to her U.S. clients; three of them were waiting for her already. The following chats ensued.

LazyBarry:
Hey love, I just rounded up with work. *whew*
I need to take the car to the mech's…he's been coughing the past days
Will buzz you when I'm back from the appointment

Miss you, daddy needs you… mwah!

iRuleMySpace1:

Lil brat…I'm here now

Coast is clear, you can come out of hiding

Frankeinstein20:

Hello

Thanks for your email at collegegrad, I hope to chat with you soon

Thoughts

iRuleMySpace1:

Tiny lizard, you better come online right now or I'll send the dogs after you

I'm not a patient one

I will whoop your ass silly

Bad dog is waiting *waiting*

I'm going to eat you to shreds

She signed in, taking her time to read her offline messages.

iRuleMySpace1:

I see you…*waiting*

woof! woof !

Butterflies:

Bad doggie *angry*

I'm not happy with u today

iRuleMySpace1:

I'm sorry…I've been busy woof

Butterflies:

U owe me money… I won't speak to you till you pay

iRuleMySpace1:

But I just need a little action before the old lady returns

Butterflies:

Pay what you owe and I'll be good to you

iRuleMySpace1:

Grrr *sad*

Send the details again

Butterflies:

So you didn't save it from the last time

iRuleMySpace1:

I have it at the office, can't bring it home

Butterflies:

Brb

Butterflies:

Hey Larry

My sweet Larry...I miss you a lot

Sorry about the car...holla when you are back

kiss *kiss*

Butterflies:

Winston Croydon

31 Jameson Park Road

Littlecountry TX 72276

$2,200

iRuleMySpace1:

This will be the second payment; I'm keeping the records if you don't

If he doesn't do the job well, I'll make sure his license is revoked

Butterflies:

I hope not, too, it will be his loss

I will move back to my apartment when renovation is completed

iRuleMySpace1:

*You're welcome to my kennel *wink**
Awoooooooooo
I'll be on my way now, give you details in a bit
kiss
Butterflies:
*You're the man! *kiss* *kiss**
She yawned from sleepiness and returned to bed.

***

Next morning she woke up to do her regular chores and returned to work. She opened her offline messages and responded to them. Waheed had been waiting.
Butterflies:
Boatguy I'm here now.
Boatman:
My habibi…I've been thinking about you
Butterflies:
*What's habibi *confused**
Boatman:
The one I love
Butterflies:
*That's nice…if you say so, I'll be your habibi *smile**
Boatman:
Good can I see you on cam?
Butterflies:
Sure…but not now…not looking really good
Boatman:
Doesn't matter
Butterflies:
I can send you pictures though
Boatman:
Fine
They both exchanged several pictures.

Boatman:

You are so beautiful honey

I'll want you more and more each day till we see

Butterflies:

Me too...you're a cute guy

I think I will come to Dubai if you insist

Boatman:

That will be awesome...gimme your dates and I'll send a ticket

Butterflies:

*Sure. *smile**

Will work something out.

Boatman:

You make me happy today habibi

I will start preparing for your coming

Butterflies:

*Awesome *yourock**

Boatman:

I will arrange for your private tutoring and also make sure you have plenty of fun

Butterflies:

I know I will...I'm really excited

Boatman:

I am too

They chatted a little more and say goodbye. Queen left messages for lazzybarry, Frankeinstein20 and iRuleMySpace1, sent the Western Union digits to the guy picking it up and drove to town an hour later to pick up $1,800, the guy having taken his cut. She changed the money to naira, bought Don a nice white T-shirt, and sent N1,000 to her mom.

CHAPTER 14

In two weeks, she had made a total of $52,000 from five clients, except Waheed, whom she developed a serious liking for. She could see through him, and he was able to win her affection. She couldn't resist his cuteness and his continuous professing of true love; this made her disclose her true identity to him. He was really exhilarated with the confession, and that made him want her more. She had given him her real phone number, her real name, added him on Facebook and followed him on Twitter.

They chatted every day and talked endlessly on the phone when Don was out. She warned him that they had to be discreet with their communication as her parents were serious disciplinarians. She showed him the mansion through her webcam, taking her laptop around the house.

"You're a rich girl," he said, having seen the size of the house, the swimming pool, tennis and basketball courts and the span of the land. "Why do you do the scam?"

"To kill boredom, sweets," she responded. "I could be very naughty."

"I love naughty, hehehe!" he said, chuckling.

Queen had traveled to Lagos with Don and spent four days with her family. He had flown to Barcelona on a quick business trip and popped in to see his family in Sweden. Queen rented a three-bedroom apartment for her parents in a newly-constructed building, furnished it and bought them a 1994 Toyota Camry. After a long meeting with her parents in their new home, they decided that her dad needed to retire from work and think of a business he could do. He came out bluntly, saying he wasn't cut out for business but would rather continue on the job he was used to. They agreed, knowing he was not good with finances. Queen promised to give him a monthly stipend to support his salary and she secretly gave her mom a million naira to expand her business.

She joined Don at a hotel on his return from the trip.

"We're going to the Caribbean in a few days, you and I. I've got some business to attend to, and it's a perfect place for a holiday," he informed her.

"For real?"

"Affirmative."

"That's some news." Very excited, Queen continuously jumped on the bed. She was not the type to hold back joy, but expressed in full. "I'm game, sweetie!"

They spent the next few days preparing, and she called her parents to inform them she would be vacationing somewhere close to the U.S. They were really happy and prayed for her. She told Waheed that she was going on research work with a team in Panama.

"I've always wanted to visit that country; you and I could go there together sometime. We'll sail in a friend's boat. Don't worry about ocean fright... I'll make you enjoy the trip," he assured her.

"I'll go anywhere with you, baby, but sailing in that much ocean... That will require a lot of guts."

"You'll be fine, trust me. First we will try with the coasts of the Emirates – before long you'll get used to it."

"OK, OK, 'til then," she agreed.

She tidied her work with clients, adjusting her story to suit the journey, and she made $6,000 before she left. On the day of their trip, two of the boys drove them to Lagos. They were joined by Charles at the airport. She flinched a little at the sight of him but simply acknowledged him to avoid Don's newly-acquired short temper.

**

At the airport, they met Short Stanley. He welcomed them, hugging the Queen very warmly.

"I've heard a lot about you, princess... this short guy always talks about you," he said, laughing and teasing Don, who slapped him on his bald head.

"You're not serious, old man. I'm quite taller than you are," Don said, defending himself. They all laughed.

All through the road trip to the hotel, Stanley never stopped talking. He kept boasting about his travels, how he knew the world and how he had connections in lots of places. Barely sitting upright, he was constantly turning around to stress his point, at times kneeling on the front passenger seat.

This guy is too much of a talker, Queen concluded in her mind. Stylishly dodging his occasional saliva-laced talks, she managed to keep a pretty face with a generous smile. She was sitting between Charles and Don, making her the direct recipient of his lousy parade. In the cool windy morning (7.25 a.m.), she fetched her sunglasses from her handbag, wearing them to cover her disdain; when he managed to make Don and Charles laugh, she joined in the façade.

***

The 80 minutes' drive from the airport eventually took them off the highway into a suburb; Stanley had been silenced by his audiences' non-response to his dry jokes. Charles had slept off from exhaustion. Their journey from Lagos had consumed a stretch of 32 hours; they connected flights in Houston; it really pleased the Queen to set foot in the United States, although she didn't show it. Now that they were in their final destination, she longed for a long soak in a hot bath and a nice clean bed to lay her head. She was not bothered about the scenery yet; there would be a lot of time to look around. She had googled the country and discovered its highlights before leaving Nigeria. And she was convinced she was going to have great fun.

They finally arrived at an old villa that was built in the '20s. The black six-feet-tall, old-fashioned gates opened, and the car made its way towards the building on a graveled road that was lined on both sides by trimmed shrubs and flowers. The massive structure built in plain design was beautified with a lot of sculpted signature. The porch had two giant beams supporting a concrete roof with carved embroidery. A lamp in the shape of a butterfly made from wrought iron hung on each beam. Butterflies were a widely recognized insignia of the isthmus.

The house butler met them and instructed two uniformed valets to carry their luggage to their rooms. The old man, dressed in an old-fashioned three-piece suit, looked like a character from the nineteenth century. Even though he was looking very frail, he maintained his composure, which almost never flinched. He acknowledged fatigue (speaking rusty English) from their long flight and promised to show them around when they had had enough rest. He personally showed them to their rooms.

"The baron will be back late afternoon and you can meet at dinner. 'Til then, please make yourselves comfortable."

The long oak dining table, so big it equated the circumference of a limousine, had 16 antique chairs. A massive crystal chandelier dressed with colored gems and small smelted rods hung five feet above the center of the table. A giant-sized painting of the last supper hung on the wall parallel to the table. At the end of this wall was a door-less arch that led to the kitchen. Two maids stood close to this arch waiting to attend to the guests.

Three minutes after they settled in, the baron walked in and was introduced by the butler as Signor Antonio Rodríguez. A six-foot-two-inch tall middle-aged man, obese with big breasts that moved freely under his silk shirt and suspenders, he was of Red Indian descent. His glossy black hair was curly and firm from heavy use of gels. His big fat hands were crested with simple gold rings on both little fingers and a large platinum ring on his right wedding finger. He welcomed them, speaking good English that was heavily saturated in a Spanish accent and a voice as husky as his size.

"Welcome to my humble abode. I recently acquired it from an old heiress whose mother was a contractor when the canal was first built. She never had kids but always welcomed a lot of visitors at home, especially tourists. She fed them for free and housed them through their entire stay. She never advertised, but her guests received her hospitality based on referral. She stopped working two decades ago but lives on royalties earned from her private islands. She has relocated to one of them and hopes to move to the afterlife from there."

"That's some story, Mr. Rodríguez," Stanley said, digging into his roasted turkey.

"I was lucky to have the money for it. Grand houses like this cost a fortune, but I was able to broker a deal of \$2.5 million. Real estate in Panama is on the rise, and the business is quite profitable."

"Interesting…" Don said and sipped some wine. "I want to know more."

"With Antonio, Panama real estate and other businesses are on lockdown. He's the best ally you can have down here," Stanley said, with a mouthful.

"My lucky day… I'll look around town and let you know what my interests are. I have this feeling that I'll be making a fortune in this country," Don dropped, smiling mischievously.

They talked business opportunities and real estate. Queen soon shifted the talks toward beaches and other attractions. One of the valets was summoned by their host and assigned to draw a timetable for the guests. He fetched some tour manuals and returned to the table. He worked with Queen, and they came up with a plan.

For the next two weeks, the best days of their lives, they toured as many beaches and archipelagos as possible, eating artfully-served local cuisines. They mixed easily with the locals and other tourists at all their destinations, learning varied cultures and partying every day. The Queen became pregnant, the news thrilled Don, and they decided to keep it low for the few days they had left in the country. They rented a beautiful four-bedroom bungalow on one of the best beaches in Panama.

Contadora Island was not a party-hardy location but boasted of being the safest in the country. The views were great, and the islanders – who mostly were foreigners – moved around in golf carts and boats, a perfect place to unwind.

The Queen returned home from a nearby island on a boat one afternoon; the boys were out for business, and she went to visit some friends. From a distance, she saw three black SUVs parked in front of the house, a couple of hard-looking guys wearing dark clothes and wielding guns. She eased the speed of the boat and changed course. She stopped the boat at a fair distance to the house where she had a clear view. From here, she saw Don, the two other guys and Mr. Rodríguez being hurled into the automobiles. Two of the guys in dark clothes were carrying a large metal box behind them, and the only guy in jeans and a T-shirt was carrying a robust duffle bag.

They had scammed a drug lord… it went bad.

CHAPTER 15

Carlos Hernandez de Bastidas was very angry. Two things got him upset. The first was that Rodríguez and Don had scammed him. He couldn't believe that he had fallen easily for it. The other was that the local press had heard of it, and the news was spreading fast. He was afraid the international press would have the news before long.

Carlos had led his mob for 30 ruthless years and he was gravely feared. Easily identifiable as a dreadful criminal, he wore a large scar across his left eye socket, from his forehead down to his left cheekbone. He was 17 when he led a group of four teenagers, saving the life of a drug dealer in his town from a machete attack by a rival gang. He sustained deep cuts on his arms and on his face, giving him his lifelong signature.

This incredible heroic act earned him interests with every single gangster that heard his story. Twenty years down the line, he pitched tent in peaceful Panama and became the biggest baron in the isthmus.

His gang oversaw every single shipment that crossed the country to North America. He was also involved in major oil thefts across Africa and Asia, gambling chains and real estate.

***

Queen was lost. This wasn't Nigeria. She couldn't even picture for real where she was. Contadora Island was agog with activities, but she was foreign. Who would she reach for assistance? Where would she start? After Don and Co.'s arrest, she fled back to the island and ditched the boat. She believed it would be a good starting point to lose it. Dusk was fast on her heels, and reality dawned on her. She couldn't locate her whereabouts.

Look for a church and spend the night there. Yes, that's it! she nearly screamed, believing she had a way out. And she moved. The day's business was giving way fast to night activities. A few parties were already starting, with Rastafarians peddling their art on street corners. Queen moved. She needed to ask for directions to a local church. Turning a whole 360 degrees, she spotted a young black woman about her age and moved. Getting closer, she turned on her charm: a smile. It was a fair attempt, though, because fear had drained her.

"Hi…" she hailed the young woman.

"Yaaa…" she replied.

"Please, I wanna find a local church. Know any 'round here?" Queen asked, trying to post an identifiable foreign status with her diction.

"Huh?" came the woman's reply.

"A church, I need to get a church here," Queen tried to explain.

"Que?" (What?) she answered in Spanish, eyeing Queen for a few seconds before she walked away.

Queen could not understand. She tried another lady.

"Hello... I am Jenny. I need to see a priest, a Reverend Father. Know where I can find one?" she inquired from a stretched old lady walking a dog.

"You sure do look like you need a priest. Where you from an' what you doin' here at this time?" the lady answered.

"I, em, I..." Queen stuttered, trying vainly to work up an explanation. The lady was already down the road before Queen could get a hint of a tale to tell. She halted and shifted to a roadside shack. With just a few dollars on her, she knew she was in for trouble. It wouldn't be an easy task to attempt to use her body first. So she sat down to think.

"Halo?" a male voice called out, jolting her into fright. She turned and saw an old man wearing big metal-rimmed spectacles beaming down at her with a smile.

"Halo?" he repeated, "Augusto, *tu?*"

Queen couldn't understand but managed to smile.

"Como te llamas?" (What's your name?) *"Tu ingles?"* (Are you English?) the man whose name was Augusto asked her. The word *ingles* helped a bit. Queen was sharp to sense it.

"English?" Queen asked.

"Yaaa... ingles..." Augusto repeated.

"Oh! Yeah, I'm English sir. Yes, English."

"*Sigueme*," (*Follow me*) Augusto invited her and moved. But she didn't understand. A few steps on, the man turned and motioned that she should follow him. Reluctantly, she did. It was already dark outside.

***

Antonio Rodríguez had only a few daring men left in his mob. But he knew none of them had the guts to step out of cover. Once news of his arrest leaked, his boys went underground. They knew that Carlos was notorious for wiping out a whole mob whenever he saw real threat to his business. Across Panama, from Panama City to Colon, Darien, Herrera, Veraguas to the regions of Embera, Kuna Yala and Kuna de Madugandi, Carlos's mob had deep roots.

His reach also cut across borders to Mexico City, Colombo, Rio de Janeiro and Moscow. Antonio Rodríguez had believed that involving Don and Co. was a very wise decision. His plan was to use imported agents to scam Carlos, dump the agents later and disappear from Panama. He felt so happy and proud that later news would leak that a minor had scammed a highly feared international drug lord.

So his foreign contacts who knew Don's capacity had suggested that they both team up for the task.

***

Next morning, Queen awoke with the first streaks of dawn. She hadn't slept much. Augusto had taken her home and offered her tea, which she had graciously accepted. His wife had been nice to Queen, too. She was lucky to have gotten a bed, and moments after she had sat on it, she had slept off. Actually, Augusto's wife had indicated the bed when she had handed her the cup of tea on a ceramic saucer. Queen knew the woman wanted to hear her story. But there was none yet; at least, no story had been cooked up. She had decided to stall for time over the tea, thanking her stars for the luck that had come her way.

"*Tan…*" (So…) Gloria Sanchez, Augusto's wife began, "Where you from and what you doin' out there so late?"

Queen was still thankful. Gloria spoke better English than her husband. Queen delayed, sipping her tea slowly and trying to work up emotions. She felt drawing pity would buy her more time to work up a story. And then, she fell sideways. Gloria smiled. Taking up Queen's legs, she straightened her on the bed and patted her on the cheek.

"*Dormir bien,*" (Sleep well) she said, pulling a blanket up to her neck.

Queen was already off in deep sleep. Her tea had been laced.

***

Queen awoke to some disturbing quietness. It was like a noisy world of silence. The room wasn't the same as the one in which she had sat the previous night with Augusto's wife. It was empty except for the wooden bed in which she lay. In her head was a kind of sound she couldn't explain. It was disturbing, no doubt.

What was happening? She looked around the room, no indication of time. But it was daybreak already. How long she had slept, she couldn't tell. Headache was part of her pain. She stood up. Her legs were heavy, and she almost fell.

Managing to steady her frame, she moved to the door and turned the knob.

***

Down in the living room of a two-bedroom bungalow on Canton Avenue, a buzzer went off.

"Mario!" Joaquin called out sharply.

And a young man came running in from an adjoining room.

"The bird calls…" Joaquin dropped.

"Bueno!" (Good!) Mario exclaimed. Instantly, he sped out of the room.

Joaquin had just informed him that their captive had awoken. He, Joaquin, led a small-time gang of thieves that was involved in burglary and drug-peddling. It was a gang of five, two of them bringing in proceeds from working as pimps for tourists and a few local patrons. Mario was the most efficient member of his gang. Joaquin had just asked him to generate all information that would help them to advance to the next level. Mario was quite intelligent and he was a fast thinker. The previous night, Mario had stumbled on info that an unknown face was spotted in a downtown shack and he had sniffed around. News had spilled that Carlos's mob was on the trail of a girl who had accompanied Don from Nigeria. The mob had put up a handsome reward for anyone who would deliver her into their net.

Joaquin knew one thing about Carlos: much as he was a dreaded drug baron, he paid his promises whenever the odds were up to his neck. *Thirty thousand dollars!* Just for Queen… in his ten years of criminal activities, Joaquin was yet to see half that sum. So, he and his gang joined the manhunt.

Mario sped down the avenue on a power bike, took a side street, cut into a boulevard and leveled plain at full speed on a highway. He had to be sure his egg was still safe. Snatching Queen from Augusto hadn't been easy. Mario and Jose Sanchez had actually tailed the girl to Augusto's home and lurked in the dark until midnight before sneaking up on them to steal Queen. But Augusto knew the town well. He had kept vigil. He knew he hadn't brought Queen home unspotted. It was just so sad that before his contact could arrive from Panama City to lift Queen for delivery to Carlos, Joaquin's boys had called.

While Mario did sentry, Jose had stolen into the house, picked the lock, picked Queen and was on his way out when Augusto's shotgun brought him crashing onto the ground. Sleeping Queen sprawled beside him. The slug had been well-aimed, and it had taken Jose out at once. Calmly, Augusto had stuffed tobacco down his pipe, loaded it tight and taken his time to light it. He had sucked hard at it, drawing in a full course, while he waited for more prey to show up. He understood mobs; they never went anywhere alone.

Five minutes… ten… fifteen… twenty… Augusto rose from his wicker chair. No more… he believed. Then, he stepped out to assess the damage his shotgun had done. The gun's silencer had really helped. No neighbour could sniff anything. Actually, he had a few, the closest being about a hundred yards from his fence. As he stepped out into the clear surrounding of his courtyard, a small cottage, he screamed and shivered vehemently in the air as he was lifted high and flung far away backwards. Blood sputtered from his mouth and his eyes lay open, staring into space. The old man lay spread-eagled on the ground, three neat holes in his starched white vest.

Gloria needed no warning. Either lie down with eyes tightly closed and pretend she didn't hear the shots or bolt out of the house and into safety through the back door. Three minutes later, Mario had emerged from the shadows, picked up both Queen and the lifeless body of his former colleague and driven away in an unmarked van.

***

Queen heard soft thuds outside, approaching footsteps, and froze. The door was of a heavy metal alloy. And it had neither peephole nor keyhole. A couple of knocks sounded on the door. Queen stepped back, away from it.

"Hello?" Mario called. No response.

"Hello? I know you're in there. I've come to help you," he said to the door. Actually, he had to raise his voice a bit to be heard from inside.

Queen kept mute, frozen with fear.

"Just calm down and don't shout. I'm coming in. Like I said, I'm here to help you," Mario said. His voice was soothing – a calm youthful voice, like that of a teenager whose voice was just breaking into maturity. Slowly, the door slid open. And Queen saw daylight. She saw the young man who owned the calm voice, and stepped back. Her fright eased, at least a bit. The young man was about her age and looked harmless. Mario entered the room and shut the door. Queen noticed that the door clicked and locked automatically once it made contact with its frame. Mario sat on the bed.

"Hello…" he offered his hand, "I'm Bran. I'm sorry you had to sleep here, but there was nowhere else to keep you safe. What's your name?"

Queen kept mute, sizing him up.

"You don't wanna talk to me, I understand. Maybe cos I am a stranger, but you should know one thing… if I could locate you here, get that door and be in here, then you gotta know I can help you. You just gotta do one thing for me… trust me," Mario explained.

"Why should I?" Queen answered.

Mario rose to his feet and began to pace around the room. "Well… let's see… let's say maybe cos you got no choice."

"Who are you?" Queen asked.

"Bran. Brandon Shepard. I met you in trouble last night and I saved your neck."

"There was no trouble. I only missed my way, and a good man took me to his home."

"Well… that same *good man* fed you a little poison you didn't know about. How do you feel? Your head…"

"I've got a headache. How did you know?" Queen asked, amazed.

"When I rescued you in company with a doctor friend last night, your skin was like you got fever. Sure you took some kinda tea in that *good man's* house?"

Queen was astonished. Mario knew this.

"Well, we got no time to waste. I know you're in some kinda trouble cos the old man almost sold you last night. But I don't know why. So… until you tell me what it is, I can't help you further," he informed her and moved to the door.

"Make up your mind, I'll be back soon. Maybe with some breakfast…"

The door sprang open. Queen couldn't tell how.

"Wait! Please wait…" she quickly called after Mario, "Please help me. Get me out of here."

"I will, when I'm back."

"Please, I need to see a priest," she pleaded.

But the door had slammed shut again before she could stop it. Slumping onto the floor, she began to weep.

CHAPTER 16

Exactly ten minutes later, Mario returned. Queen rose the moment she heard the door slide open. She had wept a few minutes and drifted away in thought.

"Come, let's go see a priest," he invited her, throwing her a black cellophane bag. "Put that on, fast!" It was an order.

Queen was stunned. The door was shut, and Mario turned away to not look at her. Queen took from the bag a long black chiffon gown, gray check headscarf, big, dark sunglasses and a pair of bottle-green leather slippers. Everything fitted in. In three minutes, she had changed. Two minutes later, she was behind Mario, clutching his bosom tightly on the power bike as it sped on a highway that led out of town.

***

Mario had taken her to a safe hideout on the outskirts of Panama City. It was necessary to keep her out of sight until Joaquin could negotiate a fresh reward with Carlos. She had kept on requesting to see a priest and had begun to weep endlessly. She also rejected the food he offered her. Mario had to agree to get her a priest. She was yet to have a clear picture of her ordeal; all she knew was that she was in trouble, on the run from the people who arrested Don.

She had one big worry: Don. She couldn't bear the thought that they were separated. How Don was faring and all. She could only pray the local police would be fair to him. At that point, Queen believed that Don was in the hands of the cops. Mario had stayed with her all day, and she couldn't tell how many times she slept off. She only agreed to touch the food after Mario had eaten a good chunk of it. She managed what was left. She was saddled with the thoughts of saving Don from captivity and getting them back home in Nigeria by all means.

When she had arrived at the church the previous night in Mario's company, everywhere had seemed calm. Mario had driven her in a delivery van marked "Henchard's Groceries," and her disguise had also been changed. She wore a fitted long-sleeved pink shirt atop blue denims with tennis shoes. She was amazed at Mario's expertise with her hair. He had thrown her a baseball cap and helped her pull it farther down her face over her eyelids. Their ride to the church was safe. And the resident priest, Father George Solarte, was at the door to welcome them. Just as she stepped in while Mario unloaded groceries from the van, Queen had fallen into the priest's arms. She collapsed.

While Father George listened to her from the confession box, she thought she heard some strange sound.

"Forgive me, Father, for I have sinned," Queen began. "Truth is, I'm in trouble. I need your help. I'm from Nigeria. I came here with my uncle who just got arrested…" She paused and waited for a response. None came.

"Father… Father…" she called. No response. In the pervading silence, she could swear the priest's breathing had stopped. Then she saw it. Blood began to spread out from under the man's soutane. It spread under the chair and covered the floor of the confession box. Queen was shocked to the marrow.

"Father! Father!" she called, barely keeping her mouth from screaming. She rose, peeped into the box, and saw the priest still seated the same way as when she joined him, but his head was tilted a little. Swiftly, Queen spun around, running toward the main doors, then…

"Stop!" a male voice called out, and she froze in her tracks, not daring to turn around.

"They're waiting for you. Don't step out, please," the voice got closer, and Queen felt a hand on her elbow. She turned, and there was Father Jean Baptiste de Nascimento.

"Come with me, we've got no time to waste. Carlos's men are everywhere – they won't stop until they get you," he said.

Carlos? Who's Carlos? she wondered as she followed the priest. They ran down the aisle, through a door and into an adjoining hallway. Next, they were speeding down a very dark tunnel. Queen bumped into the man a couple of times. The tunnel was wide but of a short distance, and in three minutes, they had hit a clearing where a black unmarked sedan was waiting. Jean turned on the ignition, and the car spun to life. They heard the first few shots; he fed gas and sped the car off, pushing Queen to lay out of sight. He was sure the mob was on their way down the tunnel, after them. Then they heard the explosion, and the church went up in flames.

Later that night, when she was safely hidden in a condominium in West Panama, Father Jean told her that Father George was dead. Some hoodlum had sneaked up behind the priest and garroted him in the confession box. Father Jean was sure he was a member of Carlos' mob. He suspected that their plot was to steal into the church like an altar boy, kill Father George quietly and pick Queen up. But it had been a flopped attempt. Father Jean told her about Carlos and his mob. He also expressed that his own life was at stake. Queen was beginning to feel better, though she was certain that with all she had witnessed in such a short time, Father Jean could have only fed her half the truth.

Queen had concentrated her efforts in asking for his assistance in helping her to reach Don or Ace. The priest agreed to help her reach Ace; it was impossible with Don. He was almost sure that Don and his cohorts were dead already, but if they were alive, Carlos would have locked them up in some dungeon whilst torturing them endlessly.

That morning when Father Jean ushered her into the car, she pondered a few things.

Where was the car they used last night? Where was he taking her? Could this young priest be trusted?

"Come in," Jean Baptiste de Nascimento urged Queen. He was already behind the steering wheel of a big black Volvo and had the engine running. He knew the lady he was ushering to join him in the car was terrified. The events of the previous days had turned her almost mute. Queen couldn't tell who to trust anymore. The mob was everywhere, and they were out to get her at all cost. A few lives had gone down in just two days, all for one lousy scam deal. She couldn't tell how much Don had expected to make from it.

While they were running away from the church the previous night, she had turned and saw a priest die from a gunshot in the head. She was so scared that she fell down and had to be pulled up and dragged to safety.

She was wondering why Father Jean would go the extra mile in revealing his profile to her. He had even told her about his lineage. He was Portuguese; his ancestors had migrated to Panama. They started a big plantation. Suddenly, Father Jean's voice jolted her.

"We've got no time to waste, come in, the mob can't be far from away…"

Queen practically flew through the open car door, her gown almost drawing her down to a fall. She was replete in a nun's regalia. Father Jean wore a fresh black soutane with a white collar. Swinging the car through the big gray gates of the condominium, he drove into the early morning sunlight.

***

After three hours of driving, they arrived at a church in the province of Bocas del Toro. He took a black handbag, a small prayer book and a set of rosaries from the rear seat and gave them to Queen. She understood. Her disguise was complete. The church cook met them at the door.

"Is the Father in?" Father Jean asked him.

"He's been expecting you, Father," the cook replied, casting a sharp glance at Queen. She held the rosary rather awkwardly.

They went in through the double doors of the main entrance to the parish house. Father Ramon Francisco was in his study. The cook ushered the visitors in. Both priests embraced.

"It's just as I told you," Father Jean went straight to the point, "Assist her to connect with her people so her soul can be saved, that's all."

"That's all?" asked Father Ramon.

"That's all."

"Sure there ain't gonna be any trouble?" asked Father Ramon.

"Very sure."

"Right. When are you picking her?" asked Father Ramon.

"I don't intend to… a few days here will be OK. I'm sure, like she claimed, if her folks know where she is, they can fly her out in no time. Right?" he turned to Queen.

She nodded.

"Good. I'll be gone. Good fortunes…" he wished Queen, waving her goodbye as he left the room. Father Ramon followed him.

Tears began to cascade down her cheeks. She knew she had just lost the only person she had managed to trust. Quickly, she hurried to the door and opened it just as the two priests were stepping into the outside daylight. Hurrying after them, she saw the cook step into the hall, and she stopped. He simply moved to her, took her hand and led her into a guest room without a word. She slumped into the bed and allowed her tears to flow.

Outside, Father Jean drew Father Ramon closer as he opened his car door.

"She's pregnant, protect her well."

It was a heartfelt plea, which Father Ramon understood.

***

7:30 p.m., Queen heard light raps on her door. She rose and opened up.

"Dinner," the cook announced.

"Five minutes," Queen requested. And the cook left. She shut her door.

About five minutes later, she heard the same knock on her door and she opened up. The cook was there to take her to the dining room. She went with him, expecting to see Father Ramon. To her surprise, he was not there. She had been thinking about Father Jean and she wanted to see Father Ramon to ask about him. Her heart had truly begun to accommodate

Father Jean, the priest who had saved her life. She didn't know what the time was but she could swear it had been at least six hours since she came. She was very hungry.

"Where's the Father?" she asked the cook.

"He's out on a mission and won't be back until nightfall. If there's anything you need, you let me know," he replied, as he flipped a large white cloth off a tray to reveal its contents. She couldn't wait to devour it.

"Wait!" she called, and he halted. "I need Internet access."

"OK," he answered and left the room.

***

Grossly satisfied, Queen dragged her frame into her room after the meal. Turning around after shutting the door tight, she stopped. Staring her in the face was a laptop with its screen on idle mode. She gasped. Nearly jumping onto the bed out of a blend of excitement, she tapped the space bar and a screensaver gave way for the desktop. Swiftly, she counted off four browsers, clicked on Mozilla Firefox and logged into Yahoomail. The Internet connection was running at flash speed.

In just three minutes, she had a brief sent to Ace. Next, she logged onto Facebook. It had taken a while trying to scan through her memory for Waheed's telephone number. She took her time to explain her predicament in four Facebook messages, which she sent to him. Satisfied, she heaved a sigh of relief and fell back onto the bed, her eyes closed. At least she had sent for help, and she was sure Ace wouldn't turn her down – Waheed as well, but the question was how long she would have to wait.

***

Ace received her message. He was asleep when his cell phone had beeped a signal; an email had entered his inbox. He read through and sat back to think over it. Turning on his laptop, he opened his inbox and read through the mail again. Panama! He needed more info. His reply had a request for Queen's exact location, what actually transpired between Don and Carlos, where Don was and all other info Queen could possibly grab. He knew peril was imminent if he attempted Panama. His best bet would be to stall for time, find less dangerous ways to save Queen and not get himself in trouble.

***

Father Ramon's cook rapped on the guest room door at exactly 7:30 a.m. to usher Queen to breakfast.

"Please hold on," she said.

"Breakfast," the cook announced.

"Breakfast? I'm yet to bathe."

"You don't want keep Father Ramon waiting, do you?"

"Oh! Wait! I'm coming," she answered. There was no missing this chance she had been crying for.

Queen had woken up to find that the laptop was no longer in the room, and she had been surprised. Everyone in this country seemed to have tricks in their blood, weird tricks. It had bothered her, though, because she had woken up from a dream where she was conversing online with Waheed and had swiftly turned to grab the laptop, forgetting she had lost connection before going to bed, but the worst of reality hit her: the laptop was gone. She had just begun to brood when the cook called; now she had some excitement in her mood, since she would be seeing Father Ramon.

"You're not dressed," the cook said.

And Queen looked herself over. She was wearing her bathrobe.

"Get dressed, I'll be back," the cook instructed her and shut the door, "You're a Reverend Sister," she heard him say through the door.

Father Ramon ate quietly.

"Thanks for the hospitality, Father."

"God be praised," Father Ramon replied.

"Em… I've been wanting to ask of Jean," she said.

Father Ramon snapped a sharp glance at her.

"Father Jean, I meant to say," she apologized.

"He is good, he got home in peace," the priest replied, not raising his face from the dish before him.

Queen knew there was no room for a casual conversation with this priest. She could swear he was a conservative. Quietly, she ate her breakfast, interrupted twice by a steward who popped in to ask if she needed anything. The young man had just resumed his morning duties. Although she couldn't identify the dishes, the meal was excellent. She had gradually begun to feel better... and the foetus inside her, too.

Back in her room, the laptop was there once again. Queen smiled. She was beginning to enjoy the drama. She logged on, and Ace's message popped into view. She screamed, "Yes!" No response yet from Waheed.

Queen couldn't just wait to bathe. Ace needed info, and she had to gather and supply it fast. She left the room and went down the hallway, where she met the steward, flashing him a smile. The youth smiled back.

He was an altar boy who doubled as a steward. Queen read his mind. He would love female company, she concluded. Her charm would work on him.

"Jenny," she said, offering her hand.

"Sister Jenny," the young man replied, ignoring the handshake.

Queen took his hand and squeezed it firmly.

"Yes, Sister Jenny... from Canada. How do you do?" she asked.

"How do you do, too?" he asked. His naivety was obvious.

"Come, you don't want to miss a good chat with me. Just be a friend, a good one. Where's Father Ramon?" she asked.

"He's gone on a sick call."

"Good. Let's go," she invited him, taking his hand and pulling him toward her room. The young man was stunned.

At 16, he had played all sorts of pranks but was yet to follow a Reverend Sister into her enclosure. His objection showed in his footsteps. Queen halted, turned and looked into his eyes.

"Don't be afraid. We are safe. Where's the cook?" she asked.

"Gone shopping."

"Who else is around?"

"Only security. The washman is due in one hour."

"Good, no need to worry," she assured him and pulled him into her room.

Tristan, the young altar boy, would always recount the events of the next 40 minutes as the most memorable moments of his 16 years in life. He had supplied every bit of info he had in response to Queen's inquiry. Cajoled and deceived, he had also divulged some secrets about the church, believing he was talking to a Reverend Sister who already knew a lot. Queen had claimed she had served in Tel Aviv and been sent as an aide to the Cardinal who had been an interim Papal Nuncio to Nigeria under the Papacy of John Paul the Second.

She had therefore used that to mask her interests especially as she had to mention Nigeria often. The last ten minutes of his stay had been for sex. Deep, satisfying sex – her long-craved desire and the young man's first indulgence. A sharp pain in Queen's tummy had caused her to yelp, and in a bid to help, Tristan had rushed to a small fridge in the room and helped her with a glass of water. As he had eased her down onto the bed, she had simply pulled him down with her and roped him. At first, his naivety had stung him into instant objection, but the moment her palm found his pipe and pressed hard on it, his will was conquered.

Tristan's mind was about to blow with an imploding urge, but Queen saved him the calamity. She had gone to breakfast with nothing under the white gown she was wearing. So it was just a case of pulling the young man's pants down and pouncing on him to satisfy her yearning, and she did! Tristan had been opened to a whole new world. Exhausted, Queen fell into a deep sleep; her reply to Ace could wait.

CHAPTER 17

The deal was well negotiated. Father Ramon loved his life and wanted so much to remain alive and continue serving God. It was his conviction that criminals were not worth suffering for. It would be a foolhardy act that could lead him to scheol if he died in the course of saving a lass wanted for her sins. He, as a priest, had been called and mandated to absolve people of their sins when they willingly confessed. His role could also include saving people from damnation when they showed they really desire to be saved.

He knew Carlos too well. Before he became a priest, they had met briefly at an occasion. That was a long time back. Over time, he had followed news of Carlos's rise to notoriety in the underworld. Father Ramon knew that Carlos *loved the church* and wouldn't hurt it. But he knew also that *Carlos was money and money, Carlos!*

Carlos's men had blown up Father Jean's parish. They had also killed its resident priest. They would stop at vanity to catch their prey. Father Ramon also knew very well that Carlos's image had been messed up by a scam masterminded by an underdog and executed by "imported puppies." It was a terrible affront.

On Queen's third day at the church, two men showed up at the gates. It was about 9:30 a.m. The security man stepped out to check them in, and they flashed their badges; cops. He threw the gates wide open and they drove in. Both occupants of the brown Toyota Cressida were in plain clothes. Tristan was at the door to usher them into Father Ramon's study. Their discussion had been brief. Five minutes in all, and they were out of the church, speeding out on a highway to Veraguas. Their mission was a success, and they needed to inform Carlos. They wouldn't risk any radio message from their car or through cell phones.

Father Ramon was Mestizo by ethnicity, and he understood Panama more than his foreign colleagues did. He was born and raised there, too.

***

Queen awoke in a dark room. The aura within clearly showed that she was no longer at the parish guest room. She tried to peer around, adjusting her vision to catch the dimness. Her surroundings smelled different. So very magnificent... As she tried to feel the edge of the bed, lights came on, flooding the room. Out of reflex, she shielded her eyes from the offensive rays. The room was magnificent truly. Everything from the furniture to the huge chandeliers hanging from the ceiling to the bed, the dressing table and the flooring was of class.

The door slid open noiselessly, and Carlos stepped in, two men in heavy dark suits behind him.

"Welcome to my palace, young lady. Make yourself at home. We finally meet. I'm Carlos, the one whom your boyfriends attempted to rob," he introduced.

Queen was shocked. She froze. The name she just heard blew her brains void instantly. *Carlos!*

"I see you've heard about me, that's good. You can tell what to expect but… I'm gonna make it easy. Everything you may need is available. Clean up. I need you in my quarters in 20 minutes," he instructed her and turned to leave. Then he halted, "Sorry about the ride in the van, it's not our usual style."

He left, smartly coursing through the way his men parted for him. Queen couldn't understand.

The van, what did he mean? Queen had slept off on her bed at the parish room after lunch on the day Carlos's men had visited. She had no wind of the visit, and she was yet to know that her lunch had been laced so heavily that she had slept for long hours into the night. The two men had returned to the church at nightfall, packed her into a body bag and bundled her like a sack of vegetables into a garbage truck marked "Paint Factory Waste"! Their ride out of town had been smooth and without suspicion, and they had arrived at Carlos's castle in Los Santos. By now, news about Carlos's ordeal with scammers was already going stale.

Twenty minutes! Carlos had said. She moved to the heavy drapes that ran around the large room and began to move them. Her search revealed a door. She turned its knob, and the door opened into a bathroom almost the size of the room. Queen couldn't believe her eyes.

In trouble yet getting royal treatment?

She took her time to shower, sticking to only the water faucets and shower tap buttons she was sure she could use. Everywhere and everything was white. Dazzling white! Even the stack of fresh towels arranged neatly on a silver line... She had barely stepped back into the room to dress up when the two men returned. Carlos shouldn't be kept waiting. She left with them.

***

Two weeks after she joined Carlos, Ace had waited endlessly for further communication. Waheed only just saw her message on Facebook. But he couldn't understand it yet. It took a while before it dawned on him that his scam lover, Queen, was in deep trouble in Panama. Much as he would love to help, he couldn't fathom how and where to start. But he had to do something. Over time, it had seemed a part of him had gone missing. He had received Queen's last message two days before trouble broke out for her, and it had been some three weeks.

The men ushered Queen into Carlos's presence and they left the room. Carlos was a big-time drug lord, no doubt. Their meeting was brief. Carlos's proposal was clear. Queen should become his mistress in exchange for her freedom after two years.

"How about Don?" Queen asked, beginning to believe she had bargaining power.

"My meat... he'll be fine. Either he agrees to my terms or he'll be meat for my dogs," Carlos answered.

Queen lacked words to describe the man seated before her. He was heavy and reeked of tobacco. Behind him was a long wine cabinet with a wide assortment of drinks.

How can I sleep with this fool? she wondered. *And where is Don?*

"Please sir, I need to see Don. Tell me, is he still alive?"

"Not just alive but kicking. He's fine. He's not paying for his transgressions yet."

"I wanna see him," Queen requested.

"Shut up!" Carlos growled, turning red. "You got no business with that fool anymore. You are mine!"

Queen was stunned. The man's rebuke was sharp and unexpected.

"Now, come here!" he ordered. And Queen flinched. "Come here!" he barked, and she rose from her seat and began to back away. Carlos's voice had drawn his men's attention. They entered.

Carlos ordered them to take her to the bed.

Queen couldn't protest. She knew she had no strength against the thugs. One picked her with ease while the other got the door, and they left the room. Five minutes later, she knew what it meant to *set the stage.* The men took her to a bedroom where they tied her spread-eagled on a massive king-size bed and withdrew. Fast on their heels, Carlos entered, a white towel around his waist. Discarding his cigar on the floor, he swiftly scooped a jackknife from the top of a bedside drawer and ripped off her clothing. Against her screams of protest and plea, the brute raped her.

Before dusk that day, Carlos had slept with Queen four times. Each time, he had been on her for at least an hour, and after, he would leave to bathe while his boys would go in and check if Queen could still carry. They gave her some hard spirits each time and when she refused, they would force her to gulp it. At night, Queen was dumped in her room, her torn privates disinfected with antiseptic. Her healing would depend on her.

***

Waheed Ibn Ahmad couldn't sleep. He had never felt so concerned about a woman until Queen showed up. He couldn't believe he was fussing over a woman he was yet to meet. Money was at his disposal, and to him, there was nothing money couldn't buy. Queen's message had said a dreaded drug baron was involved, and Waheed understood what it meant. He knew the business thrived for barons and other syndicates that indulged in and patronized it. He also knew they protected their interests often with their lives. But he had money. He could buy Queen out. Picking his cell phone, he called up his travel agent and asked him to arrange his departure to Panama in three days.

**

Two black Mercedes-Benz cars drew up before the gates of Carlos' castle and got checked through by security. Pulling through, the drivers swung the cars through a long stretch of winding road to the roof of the castle, which housed the castle's major car park and helipad. It was Queen's seventh day in Carlos's house. She had lost her pregnancy on the fourth day. When Carlos went in to her on the second day and she refused him, he had beaten her and raped her several times. She was forced to ingest concentrated alcohol by his men and had been doused with various fluids to keep her conscious after she had been in almost vegetative states.

As the cars pulled to a halt in linear fashion, three men dropped from each car, wielding guns. From the rear one, a blindfolded man with his hands tied to the back was pulled out. Heavily guarded, they moved toward a flight of stairs that descended from the roof to an elevator landing just below the penthouse. All seven men got into the elevator and rode down to the first floor. There were more guards waiting in the hallway as the elevator doors swung open. The prisoner was handed over, and his receivers took him down the hallway into a conference room. Pulling the bag off his head and releasing his bound hands, they nudged him into the room and retreated.

Don shook his head. His vision was blurred and had to be cleared. At the head of the long conference table was Carlos. They had met twice already.

"Halo?" Carlos called out to him.

Don kept mute. He knew who he had come to face. "Halo?" Carlos called out again, "Ain't you gonna sit?"

Don simply moved to the opposite end from Don's position and sat down.

"Yeah, you may not wanna talk to me, I understand. About your friends? Don't worry… it's all part of the fun," Carlos said, laughing. His laughter was more of a cackle.

Before Don, Carlos had personally supervised Charles's violent killing. Don had watched Charles ripped to shreds with a chainsaw while Carlos drank brandy, relishing the scene. Charles had been dismembered limb by limb and had died during the amputation of the third limb. Yet the tormentor continued on the boss's orders until the unfortunate youth became a mass of fleshy garbage. Stanley had watched, too; he threw up a couple of times.

Don and Stanley had their heads held firmly by the boys forcing them to watch in horror while Antonio Rodríguez was laid face down and had a big hole drilled into his skull with an electric drill. He was later cut in half from his groin up to his skull.

Don was sure Stanley had been killed. He hadn't seen him since the horrific killings, and he knew it was his turn.

"Well, I got a deal for you," Carlos said, jolting him out of his reminiscence. Don just looked on.

"Meanwhile, yeah… I got a surprise for you… Henckel!" he called, and a door opened. A broad-chested, fat thug pushed in a wheelchair. Dressed in an immaculate ankle-length, white silk gown, Queen sat numb on the wheelchair. It was obvious she had been through hell.

Don sprang to his feet.

"Queen!" he screamed. He couldn't believe his eyes. In a flash, he dashed to her, knelt beside her, sobbing and grabbed her in a bear hug. Queen attempted to rise but couldn't. She was in deep pain. Carlos let the reunion last only three minutes and called again…

"Henckel!"

The thug showed up, and Queen was gone. Don knew better than to attempt to stop the thug. He could only slump to the floor in tears.

"She's your wife?" Carlos asked him, "I see you love her dearly. Oh! Splendid! Get up and sit down."

Don complied. It was an order, though it was coolly stated. Carlos approached him.

"You will have your freedom and your wife back once you pull my deal through. Henckel has the details waiting for you. You mustn't fail! It's a hundred million euros scam, and I want all the money intact in seven days… your time's counting already. Ask for anything you need, you'll get it. Once Henckel drops you at the airport, you're alone. Your wife's freedom depends on your successful return with my money."

From the door, Carlos called, "You'd love to see your friend? The bald head? Watch his video now."

Don gasped and clutched his tummy. He couldn't stand Stanley's gruesome death. By the time he mustered enough courage to straighten up, he was alone in the room.

CHAPTER 18

Waheed Ibn Ahmad flew into Tocumen International Airport on the outskirts of Panama City on a Wednesday morning. It was three days after Henckel dropped Don at the same airport on his way to Dusseldorf. Waheed had a car rental waiting for him. Luggage checking at the airport was a bit stiff. From his phone, he dialed the telephone number he was instructed to call. A voice told him he was waiting the arrival. He ended the call and moved. On stepping outside, he saw the inscription, "AHMAD," boldly held by a smartly-dressed chauffeur. Waheed smiled and raised his hand. The chauffeur, a young man of about 30, beamed a wide smile and walked to him.

"Asalam alaikum," ("Peace be unto you") he greeted Waheed, widening his smile.

"Amin! Alaikum 'salam" ("Amen! Same to you") Waheed answered, a bit surprised.

The young man took Waheed's briefcase and led the way to a car park. As they were walking, he turned twice to glance at his client. He could smell money; he knew instantly that his client was a big fish. At the car park, he held the door to a big black Cadillac and ushered Waheed in. Carefully placing his briefcase beside him, the driver entered his seat and swung the car out of the parking lot. He hummed a tune for a few minutes then stopped, punched some digits on the car's radio and it went into auto search. In about five seconds, a muezzin's call for prayer filled the car. Waheed smiled. His driver sure knew how to entertain his client.

It took about 30 minutes of driving before the driver swung the car through the gates of Treasure Island condominium on Thomas Drive. Waheed had made a reservation.

***

Ace was restless. He hadn't slept well for days. Queen's message came to him as a distress call, and though he'd sworn to forget her for good, he couldn't help but think that she needed his help. The big problem was how to get her out of Panama. He had tried to research the land, but all he could come up with was routine info. Queen hadn't sent her exact location. All he knew was that the deal with Don had backfired. He was disturbed. He believed that though she betrayed him, he considered her as a friend and deserves to be happy. He resolved to continue trying.

***

One hundred million euros!

That was the only thought that filled Don's mind. Carlos had made the venture sound easy but he was very clear about his instructions. He wanted him in Panama with all the money in seven days. As he sat in the KLM jet on its way to Düsseldorf International Airport, Germany, he began to curse the weather. Issues about climate change had been on the front burner lately, and though he gave no attention to it, he never believed he would have any business with it someday. He had three days left. Two days had been wasted; his first flight out of Boston was cancelled almost at takeoff. The control tower had simply said the weather was bad. A thick haze had been spotted in the cloud, and it was adversely affecting visibility. A plane crash was narrowly averted, and all scheduled flights for the next six hours were cancelled. Don was mad.

The time had to be extended. Don was in panic. He had landed in Amsterdam Airport, Shiphol, and connected another flight to his destination.

***

At Father Ramon's church, Tristan was confused. Father Ramon was missing and the police had no trace of his whereabouts. Tristan felt bad. He loved the priest. Father Ramon had been treating him like his own son. He was more accommodating than his predecessor who almost sacked Tristan from the church's payroll. But he had a bigger problem. Reverend Sister Jenny was gone. She left unannounced, without as much as a wink to him. He had not been able to get her off his mind since the midmorning when she had willingly brought him into adult life. He had seen a lot of porn films, but those ten minutes with Sister Jenny was the best moment of his entire life.

His torment was that Sister Jenny's picture remained in his mind. Her scent was all over him. She was so beautiful for a nun. He couldn't enter the parish house without seeing her naked body clearly before him. A number of times, he had sneaked into the guest room she used and laid on the bed with his eyes closed. Each time he relieved the events of that moment; he relished it a lot. He often ejaculated. It was very clear to him that he desired to see her again – not just to see her, but to sleep with her again.

I need to see her again. He thought to himself, grabbing his rock-hard crotch and pressing it hard to ease his discomfort.

***

5.10 a.m., Waheed woke up. His morning prayer would be at 5.30, he wouldn't miss it. Abdul, the chauffeur, had promised to check on him, and though he didn't want to waste time before starting his search for Queen, he knew he needed assistance. His mission was not one to be made public news, and Queen's message had said that some vicious gangsters were involved. He rose from his bed, entered the bathroom and began to perform his ablution.

At nine a.m., Abdul was yet to turn up. Waheed could no longer wait. It had been one week since he saw Queen's message. He dressed up and took a flight of stairs downstairs. He located a payphone at the lobby and dialed the number Abdul gave him.

"Diga?" ("Hello?") a female voice answered in Spanish.

Waheed paused. He didn't understand.

"Diga?" the voice repeated.

He cast a glance at the receiver and returned it to his ear.

"Hello," the female voice said again.

"Oh hello," Waheed answered.

"Yeah, how may I help you?"

"May I speak with Abdul?"

"Dunno any Abdul. Check the number you dialed."

"No, hold on. Get me Abdul please…" he frantically began but heard a click, and the line went dead.

He stared at the receiver in sudden confusion and hung up. He couldn't believe it. The chauffeur had said his name was Abdulmalik, a Tunisian immigrant who worked for a high profile car rental and security agency. He had promised Waheed he would help with his mission. But he couldn't understand. Abdul didn't seem real. Waheed walked toward the bar and mounted a barstool. As the bartender brought him the dry martini he ordered, it became clear to him he had used some cash. When they had arrived at the condominium, he had so generously tipped the chauffeur ten dollars. But he increased it after the guy fell at his feet with all gratitude, making promises that he would be at his beck and call all through his stay.

He had pulled Abdul to a corner of the lobby and told him he had come to Panama to find a girl who was in trouble and Abdul had revealed he had contacts that would help. That revelation had earned him two hundred dollars. Waheed sipped his drink and tried to disbelieve the truth. He beckoned to the bartender.

"How do I get the police?" Waheed asked.

The man's grin ceased. He stepped back and looked Waheed over.

"You want the police, Mister? For what?"

"A friend is in trouble. I need to help her."

"Sure you're not bringing the cops here?"

"No. Just need to report the situation."

The man left; he put a call through to his manager and got the okay before coming out. He handed Waheed a small white card. On the card was a scripted address and telephone number.

"Thank you," Waheed said and dipped his hand into his pocket but suddenly stopped. He decided he wouldn't give any more tips unless he was sure of the truth. Quickly, he went to his room, dressed in a gray suit and left the condominium. He stood on Thomas Drive, flagged down a cab and gave the cabbie the card.

"*Bueno!*" ("Good!") the man said and moved into the traffic.

***

Queen was healing fast. She had refused to resign to fate. She lived every moment, counting minutes as they ticked. Don's return was getting closer. She had no doubt that he would succeed and return with Carlos's money. Her only fear was that Carlos may not live up to his word. But as the thought worried her, she refused to entertain it. With all she had been through, she knew Carlos couldn't be trusted. But she trusted Don. Her Don won't fail to succeed. If not for anything, she was his treasure. Don had sworn to live and die for her. She eagerly awaited his return.

She had been scheming on how to take her revenge on Carlos after her freedom. She believed she had found love and also found life in Don. She had been keen to protect her pregnancy, Don's heir, with the last drop of her blood. But Carlos had killed it. Even if anything should have made Don turn against her, that pregnancy would have been her lifeline.

He deserves to die! she concluded.

Every day in the privacy of her room, she kept reciting The Lord's Prayer while watching a wall clock tick away. She was willing to go into deep supplications to God for help but she didn't know how to do that. At least, from her primary school's morning assembly, she could still remember bits and portions of The Lord's Prayer, and before the end of the first day, she could say it well.

By the fourth day, she was still alone, left without any communication. The doctor had warned Carlos strictly to leave her alone. The doctor said it would take her at least six months to recover and be ready for sex again. She was thankful to the doctor for the clever lie. She had tried to leave the room and trace Henckel, but the door was jammed. She only saw them when they wanted to see her. At times, she would sit and cry. She would remember Don, Ace, her mum, her siblings, her lost baby and her friends. Then, she would begin to cry bitterly and ask herself if that was how her life would end. She told herself that even though she betrayed Ace, he could still try to help her.

***

Don checked into Adler Hotel, Düsseldorf. It was located in a quiet area; he chose it because he wanted to keep a low profile. The ambiance was good, and it was close to a river. The hotel used to be very busy, but over time, a lot of its patronage had dropped. It wasn't far from the town center. Don's mission was a tough one, and he was already late. Two days before his arrival, he was supposed to meet a contact who was waiting to deliver a pack of Viagra. Carlos had sent the pills to Germany. He didn't trust Don, so he sent it through an agent in Tashkent, Ukraine. Don was to receive it in Germany and ensure it was delivered.

His second assignment was a set of codes, which, when decoded, would clearly state a hitch-free transfer of crude oil between Carlos and his German client for ten straight years. The codes were encrypted in a media card inside Don's cell phone. Both deals amounted to 100 million euros.

Don checked in and picked the telephone immediately. He decided against it, showered, changed his shirt and stepped into the street. Quickly, he located a restaurant, entered it, located its restroom, went in and called Giovanni, his contact. His cell phone was a CUG, created solely for the purpose of that deal. There was another problem. Giovanni, a small Italian waiter who worked for a local ticketing and reservation agency, told him he had left Düsseldorf. He had waited and tried to make contact with Don, but couldn't. He was in Zurich.

"Shit!" Don cursed, nearly smashing the phone. He had just two days left. He had to compose himself. He threw some water on his face and dabbed it well with a disposable towel before he stepped into the restaurant and ordered food. He had no appetite but he had to force himself to eat something for two reasons. The food wasn't good at the Adler, and he had to go to Zurich as soon as possible.

CHAPTER 19

Waheed got to the police station and asked to see the chief. After some questioning, he was directed to the office.

"Welcome, sir. Please sit down," the police chief said, offering him a chair.

Waheed sat and wasted no time.

"I am Waheed Ibn Ahmad from Abu Dhabi. I came here to look for a friend. She's lost in your country," Waheed said.

"Hmm…" the police officer sighed and fixed him a steady look. He picked a pencil, drew a notepad closer, placed the pencil on it and pushed both towards Waheed.

"I need all information you've got about your friend," he said and rose.

"Wait! You're not leaving? Here…" Waheed quickly halted him and brought out his cellphone, he presented Queen's photo, "That's her. Queen…"

"Queen?"

"That's her name. She came here with some friends, and they got into trouble with some of your people. I think they got arrested somewhere."

"I see…" the officer replied.

***

Don was in a bad mess. On his way to Zurich, he crossed paths with Giovanni, who took the next flight out of Zurich to return to Düsseldorf. He should have arranged a meeting before getting on the plane. They would have arranged a meeting point.

"Shit!" he cursed and smashed the phone against a wall. In anger, he left the toilet and was already in the hallway when he remembered the media card in the phone. He hurriedly got back to the toilet, removed the card from the device, and pounded the phone to as many pieces as he could before flushing it down the toilet.

He walked to a shop, bought another cellphone and called Giovanni. He had memorized all numbers he needed for the trip. Then, he took a flight back to Düsseldorf. Giovanni was waiting at Düsselstrand, a water park. Don forced his anxiety to calm. The seven days' ultimatum from Carlos was over, and he knew there was trouble. He was thinking about Queen and what Carlos might do to her. He was also thinking that Carlos might send someone after him without knowing that he was yet to receive the package. He strolled into the water park. It was a Saturday, and the place was beginning to fill up. He was hungry, but food could wait. In the park, amidst the noise from kids shouting and enjoying their games, Don walked around in search of Giovanni. He fetched his phone to call the number and suddenly, he was jolted and the phone fell off his hand. Someone had bumped into him. Before he could turn, the offender picked the phone and handed it to him with full apologies and walked away. A few seconds after, Don moved in the man's direction.

Giovanni sat on a vacant bench, wore his spectacles and began to peer through a magazine like he was straining to read the words. Don joined him.

"Sir, could you please…" he said and pointed to a picture on the magazine.

Don nodded.

"Thank you," Giovanni said. A few minutes later, he rose and left. Don noticed a small black bundle where Giovanni had sat and picked it up.

"Hold on, sir," he called after Giovanni, "You left your…" he continued and ran after the Italian. But the small man was gone. He had done his job. Still running after Giovanni, he left the park. It was time to go for the 100 million euros. His next contact was Yuri Karpov. Don called him and gave him his location. In ten minutes, Yuri arrived. He was a smartly-dressed chauffeur who came with an airport taxi. He worked for Herr Helmut Albrecht . Yuri drove the black Mercedes-Benz around in a wide arc, flashed his headlamps twice and beeped his horn once. Don got the signal and moved down the street. Yuri approached with the car, and Don flagged him down. He rolled down his window, and Don bent to speak to him.

"Airport," Don said.

"Right," Yuri answered, "Hop in, Mister…"

Don entered. It was a well-arranged signal. The moment Don bent to say his destination, Yuri had seen the 'C' on a small round pendant hanging from a gold necklace around his neck. It confirmed he was the man Carlos. Yuri pulled into the traffic. They had about 30 minutes between them and Helmut Albrecht's home. Yuri had been on patrol for four days, waiting for Don to make contact. He knew that the German drug lord, Albrecht was infuriated.

Herr Helmut Albrecht was a man with a rash temperament. He was of the old German blood, with the belief that the blood of a German is superior to that of every other human being. He hated Blacks and would give anything to see them extinct. His father had died during the Second World War; his mother was arrested and tortured for helping some soldiers on a Peace-Keeping operation. She was released later but was found dead a week later; her crotch had traces of blood, and scratches on her skin showed she fought against her abusers before she was overpowered.

Helmut's only brother, who worked as a double agent, was accused of treason in Moscow and jailed for three years in Lubyanka prisons. The day after he was released, he was shot dead on the streets of Moscow by a teenage girl who turned herself in to the police and explained that she had just taken her revenge on the man who killed her mother. Helmut Albrecht was 28 years old then. He had begun a solitary life on the streets of Berlin, trying to eke out his livelihood by all means. He had a college degree in psychology and worked as a college professor for five years before joining the army. He was dismissed ten years later. His hatred for the Black race was unmatched, and his blood was filled with incurable racism.

Yuri drove through the gates of the mansion, which rolled open on their own. He stopped for a check. An electronic scanner certified the car OK, and a security officer checked Don's papers before waving them on. Ten yards up the driveway, Don noticed some Rottweilers and men in suits perched under some well-tended trees. He turned as Yuri drove on and managed to count. *Thirteen dogs and four men!* Goose bumps broke all over him instantly. Aside from the dogs and men, there was no sign of life anywhere around. The young Russian stopped the car about ten meters to the front of the building and nodded Don to get out. Don was confused.

"You've kept the baron waiting for too long. Get out!" he barked, and Don shook. He slipped out of the car and was barely standing on his feet when Yuri rolled the car around and sped down the driveway. Don turned with the car's motion and stared at it as it went away. He couldn't tell how long he was there, but as he woke up and came to his senses, a sickening ache at the back of his head didn't allow him to raise it well. He managed to look around and saw that he was in a fairly-lit room. He was lying on a couch. He sat up and felt the back of his head. There was a slight bulge that ached. He rubbed it a few times before he heard a baritone voice and stopped.

"That's just a taste of things to come. You're an idiot!" Herr Helmut Albrecht spat at him, swaggering into the room, "You kept me waiting… four days! You'll die here!"

Don began to shiver. The man before him didn't look like a normal fraudster. Something about the air around him smelled sinister.

"Get up!" Albrecht growled. As fast as he could, Don rose to his feet. But he shook and almost fell. He was feeling numb from the ache in his head and he was very hungry.

"Sit on the floor!" Albrecht ordered him, and he complied.

Though he was terrified, he was beginning to hate Albrecht. Henckel had simply told him that Helmut Albrecht was an ex-soldier, so he should be careful in dealing with him. Henckel didn't tell him about the man's beastly temper. He thought that because he had also been in service, Albrecht wouldn't be tough to handle. He had not only delayed in getting to Albrecht's home, he had gotten there and stood staring at the leaving car until a guard clubbed him at the back of his head.

The moment Albrecht had seen him on the screen when he entered Yuri's Mercedes-Benz, he wanted him dead. Carlos didn't tell him he was sending a Black guy to him. In all his years as a gangster, he had carefully avoided dealing with Blacks. He thought that Don was not just Black but also an incompetent fool.

"Where's my oil deal?" Albrecht roared.

Don dipped his hands into his pockets, but his cellphone was not there.

"My phone... my cellphone..." he stuttered.

"Jan!" Albrecht barked, and instantly, a fifty-something year-old eunuch entered the room with Don's cellphone. Grabbing Don, he pulled him towards a reading desk, pushed him into a chair and dropped the phone on the desk. Quickly, Don removed the media card and presented it to Albrecht . Jan tapped a laptop on the desk, and its screen came on. He inserted the card into a card reader and pushed it into a port. Albrecht drew close towards Jan, who accessed the card and saw only a set of codes.

"Codes?" Albrecht asked Don, calming down and pulling a chair to sit down.

"It's encrypted. Carlos thought it was safer that way," Don answered.

"Then decrypt it!" Albrecht barked, banging a heavy fist on the desk.

That shook Don. Jan pushed the laptop to him, stepped out and returned with a glass of water, which Don gratefully accepted and downed in one long gulp. In fifteen minutes, he had decrypted the codes. He didn't do it himself; in the media card was a software which he had quickly installed. The software was an auto-decrypter, and immediately after using it, he had uninstalled and deleted everything about it before turning the screen towards Albrecht .

For the first time since he met Albrecht , he saw the German lord smile. He was reading the terms of the oil deal, which looked too good to be true. In exchange for 100 million euros, he would have access to a weekly supply of one million barrels of Nigerian crude oil for ten uninterrupted years. He had to also assassinate a disturbing politician in the Nigerian government to seal the deal. Some foreign interests wanted him out of the way for easy dealings; he was too greedy, also. He had to kill the politician in such a way that his death would never be traced to the masterminds.

Picking up the laptop, Albrecht turned to Jan.

"Throw him out," he ordered Jan and moved to the door. Don halted him.

"The money, sir…"

Albrecht turned and gazed at him.

"The code means nothing without being activated," Don informed him.

The man turned red.

This little Black thing is playing games with me!

Swiftly, he returned to the desk and stared down at a terrified Don.

"Activate it now!"

"I can't…" Don stuttered. "I can't until he sees proof of your payment."

Albrecht was beaten. He sat down and blushed. Suddenly, he landed Don a big slap that threw him to the floor. Don winced in pain. In three seconds, Albrecht kicked him roughly in the belly eight times. He was fuming and screaming obscenities at the little man. Jan fell over Don to protect him, and Albrecht stopped and slumped into the couch.

"You kill him, sir, you lose the deal," Jan calmly reminded his boss.

Albrecht nodded a few times, pulling himself together. He took the laptop, logged into a bank account portal and gave the laptop to Don.

"His account details…" he said to Don, who was totally broken. He could taste his blood in his mouth.

Don punched in some particulars, and Albrecht handled the rest. The deal was sealed. Don told him the code was activated. Albrecht quickly flipped windows and checked the page on which the decrypted code was. A green bar bearing the word "activated" was flashing steadily on the screen.

CHAPTER 20

Queen was tensely counting time. Carlos became uneasy as the seventh day was drawing to an end. He became suspicious that Don would not return the money to him after all. He knew how much Albrecht wanted the oil deal so he was sure he would pay. He was also sure that Don's life depended on Queen. But as tension grew in him on the eighth day, he began to regret entrusting such a huge deal to him. He became furious.

Two days after Don was due to return, Carlos called Henckel.

"I guess the fool ain't coming back with my bucks? How is he?" Carlos asked Henckel.

"Bobby lost him in Zurich, but we've got an eye on Albrecht's villa. He arrived there but is yet to leave," Henckel answered.

"I sense a double-cross. Albrecht hates Blacks, but his love for oil would set his thinking right. You're not thinking he's done a deal with Don, are you?"

"He hates everything Black, sir. I don't see anything changing that."

"Love is stronger than hate. Love is stronger than blood. Love is stronger than everything! Albrecht loves oil!"

"We should expect Don's return if love is that strong, sir. He loves his woman," Henckel answered.

"I'm not so sure now!" Carlos declared.

Carlos paced the floor and paused before Henckel. He pressed a buzzer on the table. Two men entered.

"Get me Roddy, I want you out there with the next flight." Carlos told Henckel.

**

Waheed had never been so disappointed. The police officer had failed him. After three days, no info had come. He went online to look at the map of Panama. He noted major cities, provinces and towns where he could possibly look for Queen. It was a difficult task, but he was willing to undertake it. He had lost 1,000 dollars to the officer and nothing but vague promises had come out of his efforts. He began to call police stations he could reach over the telephone. He was exhausted after spending six hours. The condominium's manager called on him to check if there was trouble because it was obvious that he was tense. Waheed explained his challenge, and the manager advised him to begin to visit the stations. He suggested he should demand that the cops place a "Missing Person" advert with a handsome reward for good information. Waheed saw sense in his advice and smiled.

He called a cab agency and hired a cab for a whole day. At the first station, he offered a $5,000 reward for any information that would help him trace his friend, Queen.

***

Don woke up. It took him about five minutes to be fully aware of his environment. The last thing he knew was Albrecht holding a gun to his temple. He couldn't understand where he was. A point in his arm was hurting, and he had to keep scratching it. He groped around in the dark and knew he was in a bed. He peered into the darkness, got up and searched the walls for a light switch. He found one and turned it on. He was amazed. It looked like he was in a hotel room. He quickly put on his shirt and felt his forehead with his hand, still scratching the disturbing pinch in his arm. He felt better. The ache had subsided, although every movement he made seemed to want to bring it back. He tried the door, and it opened to a hallway. He left the room, went down the hallway and found an elevator at the end. While he waited for it, he raised his arm and looked closely at the hurting point. He could see no visible scratch and seemed to mean nothing. He took the elevator and rode to the ground floor. He stepped out, crossed the lobby and pushed past a big glass door and went outside.

***

Carlos ordered Roddy to spread Queen flat on her back on a bed and tie her. It was four days after Don's supposed return to Panama. Queen had been living in hell since the deadline. She knew Carlos too well to expect pardon. Henckel was already in Germany and he had reported that Helmut Albrecht transferred the total sum but Carlos didn't receive it. Henckel didn't know where to start. Giovanni couldn't help beyond the info he had. It became clear that Don had outsmarted them. Henckel knew better than to return to Carlos with such information. Queen tried to plead, but no way. She could tell she was about to suffer the ultimate fate. She believed that Don might have been delayed but she was devastated when she heard that Don was on the run with the money. She didn't know what to think; she couldn't believe that Don would leave her for dead. She couldn't believe she had lost everything: Ace, whom she loved, her baby, her freedom, her body ... and she was about to lose her life. Terrifying pains ripped her heart. As she was struggling against Roddy and his assistants, Carlos bust into the room, a punch-drill in his hand. Queen was fixed on the bed. She screamed at the top of her voice and kept on screaming until she could scream no more.

Carlos and his men just stood and watched her.

"You done?" he asked her.

"Please…" she pleaded, her voice frail and almost inaudible.

"He's gone," he said, cackling. "Your husband is gone. I believed he loved you, I believed he cared for you. He's gone, and my money's gone with him. He has sold you for money."

"No, Don won't do that."

"Yes he did! Where's my money? Where's my money?" he screamed and jammed the drill into her left foot, boring a hole ruthlessly through it up to her ankle.

Queen let out a high-pitched scream, shaking violently. She fainted. Carlos saw her body go lifeless and stopped the drill.

"Clear her out!" he ordered Roddy.

***

Albrecht wanted to complete the deal quickly. He had to send the Viagra to Nigeria, but first he needed to be sure of its potency. He summoned a male and female hooker; the guy took one look at the blue pills and burst into laughter.

"What's this supposed to be?" he asked Albrecht .

"Use it!" Albrecht ordered him.

"I'm good without pills!" the man added.

Albrecht was beginning to think the man was making a joke of the situation and ordered him to swallow the pills at gunpoint. He wanted to see a first-hand reaction and watch them have uncontrolled sex under the influence of the stimulant. Albrecht spent the longest ten minutes of his life waiting for the reaction. The blue pills were supposed to contain a mixture of cyanide, another non-traceable lethal substance and Viagra. Carlos knew that the senator received a constant supply of the best Viagra from Europe, which he regularly used to boost his dying sexual vigour. Albrecht knew about this too. He wasn't interested in the sexual entertainment between the two but he wanted to see the man die in the exact stated time. If the pills had been well packaged as planned, one pill would kill a victim in less than three minutes. He forced the young man to swallow more. The guy protested, and he raised his gun. The guy gulped down an overdose yet nothing happened. Albrecht went mad.

"Jan!" he yelled and Jan came in.

"The laptop!"

Jan brought him the laptop, and he quickly tried to assess the digital confirmation of the transaction. He was shocked at what he saw: a clown's face bouncing all over the screen like a Ping-Pong ball. In terrible fury, he smashed the laptop on the floor. Snatching up his gun, he shot Jan on the forehead. Next, he shot the two hookers, and that begun the shooting frenzy.

***

As the sun set on a vast open landmass, a white unmarked van drove at full speed along the empty dirt road, leaving a long cloud of dust behind it. It screeched to a halt at the edge of a dumpsite and reversed a few meters onto the heap of rubbish. The back doors swung open, and a wake of vultures abandon a decaying dog they were feeding on, flapping their large wings in flight. Two men leaped out of the back of the van onto the pile. They look around and when they were sure the coast was clear, got back into the van and dragged the lifeless body of a woman onto the heap and got back in the van. "I need to take a leak," one said and jumped back on the heap. He unzipped and eased himself over Queen's body, mostly on her frail face. He zipped up when he was done and got back into the van, which sped off immediately, raising dust as it went.

***

The Boeing 777 jet landed in Accra at exactly 18.20 hours GMT, a few minutes later, Don stepped out into the early evening. He wasn't going back to Nigeria, at least not yet. The morning after his ordeal with Albrecht, he had taken a mid-morning express out of town. He had booked a flight to Nigeria that would make a stop-over in Accra. There was no going back to Carlos; that was suicide. It would also be easy for him to be found in Nigeria. He thought about his home in Benin, his gang and what would become of them.

He thought through his ordeal since leaving Nigeria and imagined how lucky he was. He would miss Queen. His worst pain was that he couldn't imagine what manner of death Carlos would give her. It also dawned on him that as long as Carlos was alive, he would remain a fugitive. He also remembered Ace, who might come asking questions about Queen.

***

Waheed had left Panama after a long, unsuccessful search for Queen; his work had got badly affected with his absence. His insistence had only cost him money with the police as they kept demanding unreasonable amounts from him in the course of their futile search. He began to realize he barely knew her and had to get back to the world that worked.

***

Architect Kofi Mensah sat in a hospital waiting area. He needed to see a medical consultant fast. He was holed up in a hotel in Takoradi and he loved the area. He had begun plans to build a seaside chalet that would overlook the Atlantic Ocean. He had a strong urge to make contact with home but he resisted it. He had also shelved the guilt of leaving Queen in trouble. His joy always returned whenever he remembered his wife and kids. His arch-enemy didn't know about them, so they were safe. Some days after he arrived at Takoradi, he had begun to feel sick and he blamed it on change of environment.

One week later, his health became worse. His blood seemed to be drying up fast, and his skin colour was changing. It was becoming a big problem for him to eat as he was constantly losing his appetite and throwing up. He quickly cooked up a new identity with which he went to the hospital. After the first series of medical tests, the lab results showed his blood had been poisoned. The first consultant told him there was no remedy. He was suspecting the patient would develop leukemia. Someone had given him a shot of a blood cancer-causing substance, and it had spread too fast through his bloodstream. He was dying slowly. He needed instant blood transfusion, but even with that, the consultant had expressed his doubts of his survival.

He left some things unsaid. He couldn't imagine when and where that happened. He kept on thinking and asking questions until he remembered the itchy feeling he had on his arm. Shocked, he paused for a minute, and it seemed reality had just hit him.

Helmut Albrecht!

***

As the vultures hovered above the Queen's motionless body, an amount of urine flowed through her nose into her lungs. It choked her, made her cough feebly and gasp for air.

The End!